AN ADAPTED CLASSIC

The Grapes of Wrath

John Steinbeck

GLOBE FEARON
Pearson Learning Group

Adapter: Earle Rice, Jr.
Project Editor: Kristen Shepos-Salvatore
Editorial Supervisor: Sandra Widener
Editorial Assistant: Kathleen Kennedy
Production Editor: Alan Dalgleish
Marketing Manager: Sandra Hutchison
Art Supervision: Patricia Smythe
Electronic Page Production: Luc VanMeerbeek
Cover and Interior Illustrator: James McDaniel

ISBN: 0-8359-1885-8
Printed in the United States of America

17 18 19 20 V036 15 14 13 12

Globe
Fearon

Pearson Learning Group

1-800-321-3106
www.pearsonlearning.com

CONTENTS

ABOUT THE AUTHOR

John Steinbeck (1902-1968), a short-story writer and novelist, was born in Salinas, California. He spent most of his life there. Steinbeck started working when he was very young. He went to Stanford University and studied marine biology. He dropped out to work his way to New York City through the Panama Canal.

While he traveled, Steinbeck did a variety of jobs to support himself. He worked as a newspaper reporter, as a worker in a trout hatchery, and as a fruit picker. He also worked in construction, on ranches, and in a biology lab. It was during this period of his life that Steinbeck wrote his first few books. Even though some of these books were considered failures, he continued to write.

Tortilla Flat (1935) and *In Dubious Battle* (1936) gave Steinbeck his reputation as a writer. *Tortilla Flat* is about the Mexican-Americans of Monterey. *In Dubious Battle* is about a violent strike among California fruit pickers. Another important work by Steinbeck is *Of Mice and Men* (1937), about a simple-minded man named Lennie and his friend and protector, George.

Steinbeck's greatest work was *The Grapes of Wrath* (1939), for which he was awarded the Pulitzer Prize. This book makes an important statement about society, and how it can work against itself. However, it is also a beautiful story about the strength of the human spirit.

After *The Grapes of Wrath,* Steinbeck wrote about sea life. With Edward F. Ricketts, he co-authored *Sea of Cortez.* He also wrote *The Log from the Sea of Cortez.* The second book is a version of the *Sea of Cortez* that includes a biography of Edward F. Ricketts. Ricketts appears again in Steinbeck's work as the leading character in the novel *Cannery Row* (1945). The sequel to *Cannery Row* was *Sweet Thursday,* about a group of poor but happy drifters who seem satisfied with their simple lives.

Steinbeck wrote a number of other books and screenplays during his life. He became known around the world in 1962, when he was awarded the Nobel Prize for Literature.

ADAPTER'S NOTE

In preparing this edition of *The Grapes of Wrath,* we have kept as close as possible to John Steinbeck's original words and style. We have changed some of the vocabulary. We have also shortened some chapters.

Some of the footnotes explain hard words. Other footnotes fill in historical details of the story.

HISTORICAL BACKGROUND

The members of the Joad family in *The Grapes of Wrath* are victims of the Dust Bowl storms of the 1930s. The Dust Bowl refers to an area of the United States that covers parts of Kansas, Colorado, New Mexico, Oklahoma, and Texas. From 1933 to 1939, dust storms and dry weather destroyed the farmlands of this area.

The early 1930s were a time of terrible drought in the southern Great Plains. Temperatures of over 100 degrees dried and cracked the earth. When the winds of 1934 began, the dried up land simply blew away into great clouds of dust. In 1933, there were 14 dust storms. In 1935, there were 40. And in 1938, there were 61.

Over 850 million tons of earth were lost to the winds. The farmers who had depended on the land for food and work were forced to look for work elsewhere. In the Depression years of the 1930s, this was not easy. This natural disaster turned successful farmers and their families into homeless and starving people.

Steinbeck wrote *The Grapes of Wrath* when people were looking for answers to serious economic problems in America. The President of the United States at that time was Franklin Roosevelt. He hoped that his economic plan, called the New Deal, would pull the country out of the Great Depression. That was two years before the attack on Pearl Harbor brought the United States into World War II.

Other writers during that time were Ernest Hemingway, F. Scott Fitzgerald, Hart Crane, Thomas Wolfe, Thornton Wilder, John Dos Passos, and Pearl S. Buck. Some of these people wrote about the same kinds of things Steinbeck did, such as the struggle for economic security and the importance of family.

PREFACE

After you finish reading this book, you might want to watch the movie version of *The Grapes of Wrath*. Released in 1940, this movie stars Henry Fonda as Tom Joad. You might also enjoy the photographs of Dorothea Lange. She recorded the history of the Dust Bowl refugees in a series of touching photographs. In Lange's subjects, we can see people just like the Joads. In their faces, we can see their suffering.

CHARACTERS

TOM JOAD
>Son of Ma and Pa Joad

MA JOAD
>The guiding, controlling force of the Joad family

PA JOAD
>A tenant farmer for 40 years who has just lost his farm to big business and the dust storms in Oklahoma

GRAMPA AND GRANMA
>The original settlers on the 40 acres that Pa Joad has just lost

JIM CASY
>A former preacher who goes with the Joads to California

ROSE OF SHARON (ALSO ROSASHARN)
>Tom Joad's sister, who is recently married and pregnant

CONNIE RIVERS
>Rose of Sharon's husband

MULEY GRAVES
>A neighbor of the Joads who refuses to leave his land

IVY AND SAIRY WILSON
>Migrants from Kansas who travel with the Joads for a while

NOAH JOAD
>Tom's older brother

AL JOAD
>Tom's 16-year-old brother

RUTHIE AND WINFIELD JOAD
>The two youngest Joad children, ages 12 and 10

MR. AND MRS. WAINWRIGHT
>The couple living in the opposite end of the boxcar where the Joads live for part of their time in California

AGGIE WAINWRIGHT
>The Wainwrights' daughter, who gets engaged to Al Joad

Chapter 1

To the red country and part of the gray country of Oklahoma, the last rains came gently. They did not cut the scarred earth. The plows crossed and recrossed the rivulet[1] marks. The last rains lifted the corn quickly, and scattered weed colonies and grass along the sides of the roads. The gray country and the dark red country began to disappear under a green cover. In the last part of May, the sky grew pale. The clouds that had hung in high puffs for so long in the spring dissolved.

The sun flared down on the growing corn day after day until a line of brown spread along the edge of each green leaf. The clouds appeared, and went away, and in a while the clouds did not try anymore. The weeds grew darker green to protect themselves. They did not spread anymore. The surface of the earth crusted, a thin hard crust. As the sky became pale, so the earth became pale, pink in the red country and white in the gray country.

In the water-cut paths, the earth dusted down in dry little streams. Gophers' digging started small avalanches. As the sharp sun struck day after day, the leaves of the young corn became less stiff. They bent in a curve at first. Then, as the central ribs grew weak, each leaf tilted down. Then it was June, and the sun shone more fiercely. The brown lines on the corn leaves widened and moved in on the central ribs. The weeds frayed back toward their roots. The air was thin and the sky more pale. Every day the earth grew more pale.

---

1. **rivulet** small stream

In the roads where the teams of horses moved, where the wheels plowed the ground and the hooves of the horses beat the ground, the dirt crust broke and the dust formed. Every moving thing lifted the dust into the air. A walking man lifted a thin layer as high as his waist, and a wagon lifted the dust as high as the fence tops. A car boiled a cloud behind it. The dust was a long time in settling back again.

When June was half gone, the big clouds moved up out of Texas and the Gulf, high heavy clouds—rainheads.[2] The men in the fields looked up at the clouds and sniffed at them and held wet fingers up to sense the wind. The horses were nervous while the clouds were up. The rainheads dropped a little spattering of rain and hurried on to some other country. Behind them the sky was pale again, and the sun flared. In the dust there were drop craters where the rain had fallen, and there were clean splashes on the corn, and that was all.

A gentle wind followed the rain clouds, driving them on northward. The wind softly clashed the drying corn. A day went by and the wind grew, steady, unbroken. The dust from the roads fluffed up and spread out. It fell on the weeds beside the fields, and fell into the fields a little way. Now the wind grew strong and hard, and it worked at the rain crust in the corn fields. Little by little, the sky was darkened by the mixing dust. The wind felt over the earth, loosened the dust, and carried it away.

The wind grew stronger. The crust of the earth broke, and the dust lifted up out of the fields and drove gray clouds into the air like sluggish smoke. The wind hit the corn and made a dry, rushing sound. The finest

---

2. rainhead rain cloud

dust did not settle back to the earth now. It disappeared into a darkening sky.

The wind grew stronger, rushed under stones, carried up straws and old leaves, and even little clods of dirt. The air and the sky darkened and through them the sun shone redly, and there was a raw sting in the air. During the night, the wind raced faster over the land and dug over the rootlets of the corn. The corn fought the wind with its weakened leaves until the roots were freed by the prying wind. Then each stalk settled wearily sideways toward the earth and pointed the direction of the wind.

The dawn came, but no day. In the gray sky, a red sun appeared, a dim red circle that gave a little light, like dusk. As that day advanced, the dusk slipped back toward darkness, and the wind cried and whimpered over the fallen corn.

Men and women huddled in their houses, and they tied handkerchiefs over their noses when they went out, and wore goggles to protect their eyes.

When the night came again, it was black night. The stars could not pierce the dust, and the window lights could not even spread beyond their own yards. Now the dust was evenly mixed with the air. Houses were shut tight, and cloth wedged around doors and windows, but the dust came in so thinly that it could not be seen in the air, and it settled like pollen on the chairs and tables and dishes. The people brushed it from their shoulders. Little lines of dust lay at the door sills.

In the middle of the night, the wind passed on and left the land quiet. The dust-filled air muffled the sound completely. The people, lying in their beds, heard the wind stop. They lay quietly and listened deep into the stillness. Then the roosters crowed, and their voices were muffled. The people stirred restlessly in their beds and wanted the morning. They knew it would take a long time for the dust to settle out of the air.

In the morning the dust hung like fog, and the sun was as red as ripe new blood. All day the dust sifted down from the sky, and the next day it sifted down again. An even blanket covered the earth. It settled on the corn, piled up on the tops of the fence posts, piled up on the wires. It settled on roofs and blanketed the weeds and trees.

The people came out of their houses and smelled the hot stinging air and covered their noses from it. And the children came out of the houses, but they did not run or shout as they would have done after a rain. Men stood still and silent by their fences and looked at the ruined corn. Women looked out from houses and wondered if their men would be able to survive this loss. It was drying fast now, only a little green showing through the film of dust. And the women came out of the houses to stand beside their men—to feel whether this time the men would break.

The women studied the men's faces secretly, for the corn could go, as long as something else remained. The children stood nearby and sent exploring senses out to see whether men and women would break. After a while the faces of the watching men lost their puzzled look and became hard and angry and resistant. Then the women knew that they were safe and that there was no break. And the children knew. Then the women asked, What'll we do? And the men replied, I don't know. But it was all right. The women and children knew deep inside that no misfortune was too great to bear if their men were whole.

As the day went forward, the sun became less red.

It flared down on the dust-blanketed land. The men sat in the doorways of their houses. Their hands were busy with sticks and little rocks. The men sat still—thinking—figuring.

Chapter 2

A huge red transport truck stood in front of the little roadside restaurant. The exhaust pipe muttered softly. An almost invisible haze of steel-blue smoke hovered over its end. It was a new truck, shining red. Twelve-inch letters on its sides spelled out OKLAHOMA CITY TRANSPORT COMPANY. Its double tires were new, and a brass padlock stood straight out from the big black doors.

A man walking along the edge of the highway crossed over and approached the truck. He walked slowly to the front of it and looked at the *No Riders* sticker on the windshield. For a moment he was about to walk on down the road. But instead, he sat on the running board on the side away from the restaurant.

He was not over 30 years old. His eyes were very dark brown. His cheek bones were high and wide, and strong deep lines cut down his cheeks, in curves beside his mouth. His upper lip was long, and since his teeth stuck out, the lips stretched to cover them, for this man kept his lips closed. His hands were hard, with broad fingers and nails as thick and ridged as little clam shells. The space between thumb and forefinger and the palms of his hands were shiny with calluses.

The man's clothes were new—all of them, cheap and new. His gray cap was so new that the visor was still stiff. His suit was of cheap gray hardcloth and so new that there were creases in the trousers. His blue shirt was stiff and smooth. The coat was too big, and the trousers too short, for he was a tall man. The coat shoulder peaks hung down on his arms, and even then the sleeves were too short and the front of the coat

6

flapped loosely over his stomach. He wore a pair of new tan shoes of the kind called "army last," with half-circles like horseshoes to protect the edges of the heels from wear.

Soon, a gum-chewing truck driver came out of the restaurant and walked over to the big red truck. The hitchhiker stood up and looked across through the windows. "Could ya give me a lift, mister?"

"Didn't you see the *No Riders* sticker on the wind-shield?"

"Sure—I seen it. But sometimes a guy'll be a good guy even if his boss makes him carry a sticker."

The driver glanced warily toward the restaurant and said, "Scrunch down on the running board till we get around the bend."

The hitchhiker flopped out of sight and clung to the door handle. It was a mile to the first turn in the road, then the truck slowed down. The hitchhiker stood up and slipped into the seat.

Out on the highway the driver squinted ahead and built up the speed of the truck a little. "Going far?"

"Uh-uh! I'd have walked if I wasn't pooped out."

"Looking for a job?" the driver asked.

"No, my old man got a place, 40 acres. He's a crop-per,[1] but we been there a long time."

The driver looked at the fields along the road where the corn was fallen sideways and the dust was piled on it. "A 40-acre cropper and he ain't been dusted out and he ain't been tractored out?"[2]

---

1. **cropper**   sharecropper; a farmer who is given seeds and lives on the land in exchange for a share of the crop.
2. **tractored out**   farmers who are replaced by tractors; may also refer to tractors that cut through farmland, destroying the houses in their paths.

"I ain't heard lately," said the hitchhiker.

"Croppers going fast now," the driver said. "One cat[3] takes and shoves ten families out. How's your old man hold on?"

"Well, I ain't heard lately. I never was no hand to write, nor my old man neither." He added quickly, "But the both of us can, if we want."

"Been doing a job?" the driver asked, continuing his investigation.

"Sure have," said the hitchhiker.

"Thought so. I seen your hands. Been swinging a pick or an ax or a sledge. That shines up your hands. I notice all stuff like that. Take a pride in it."

The hitchhiker stared at him. "Like to know anything else? I'll tell you. You ain't got to guess."

"Now, don't get sore. I wasn't getting nosy. I just like to notice things. Makes the time pass."

"I'll tell you anything. Name's Joad. Tom Joad. Old man is ol' Tom Joad." His eyes rested broodingly on the truck driver.

"Don't get sore. I didn't mean nothing."

"I don't mean nothing neither," said Joad. "I'm just trying to get along without shoving nobody around." He looked out at the dry fields.

The driver chewed his gum and waited until the air seemed neutral again. "Guy that drives a truck does screwy things. He got to. He'd go nuts just setting here."

"Must be tough," said Joad with no emphasis.

"Well, it ain't no cinch," the driver said testily.

"You're all wound up," said Joad. "What's the matter—got a girl?"

"Well, sure. But mostly I want to get ahead. I been

---

3. cat Caterpillar brand tractor

training my mind for a long time."

Joad interrupted. "I ain't got much further to go."

The driver went on quickly. "I train my mind all the time. I took a course in that two years ago. Now I try to remember everything about people I meet. Kind a clothes, an' shoes, an' hat, an' how they walk, an' maybe how tall, an' what weight, an' any scars. I do it pretty good. Sometimes I think I ought to take a course to be a fingerprint expert. You'd be surprised how much a guy can remember."

After a long pause, Joad chuckled silently and said, "You sure took a long time to get to it, buddy."

The driver did not look over. "Get to what? How do you mean?"

Joad's voice became harsh. "You know what I mean. You know where I come from." The driver was silent. "Don't you?" Joad insisted.

"Well—sure. That is—maybe. But it ain't none of my business. I ain't a nosy guy."

"The hell you ain't," said Joad. "That big old nose of yours been sticking out eight miles ahead of your face. You had that big nose going over me like a sheep in a vegetable patch."

"You got me all wrong—" the driver began weakly.

"No, mister, you got me all wrong," said Joad. "Sure I been in McAlester.⁴ I ain't keeping quiet about it. Been there four years. Sure, these is the clothes they give me when I come out. I don't care who knows it. An' I'm going to my ol' man's place so I don't have to lie to get a job."

"That ain't none of my affair."

"Nothing ain't none of your affair except driving this here rig along, an' that's the least thing you work

---

4. **McAlester**   the state prison at McAlester, Oklahoma

at. Now look. See that road up ahead?"

"Yeah."

"Well, I get off there. Sure, I know you're busting your britches to know what I done. I ain't a guy to let you down." The high hum of the motor dulled and the song of the tires dropped in pitch. The truck drifted to a stop where a dirt road opened at right angles to the highway. Joad got out and stood beside the cab window. The exhaust pipe puttered up its barely visible blue smoke. Joad leaned toward the driver. "Homicide," he said quickly. "That's a big word—means I killed a guy. Seven years. I'm out in four for keeping my nose clean."

The driver's eyes slipped over Joad's face to memorize it. "I never asked you nothing about it," he said. "I mind my own yard."

Joad smiled and slapped the metal door with his palm. "So long, fellow. You can tell about it in every truck stop from here to Texola. Thanks for the lift."

For a moment the driver stared after him, and then he called, "Luck!" Joad waved his hand without looking around. Then the motor roared up and the gears clicked and the great red truck rolled heavily away.

Chapter 3

Joad turned around and faced the dusty side road that cut off at right angles through the fields. The sun was hot, and no wind stirred the dust. He slipped off his shoes and worked his damp feet comfortably in the hot dry dust until little spurts of it came up between his toes. He took off his coat and wrapped his shoes in it and slipped the bundle under his arm. And at last he moved up the road, shooting dust ahead of him, making a cloud that hung low to the ground behind him.

Farther ahead of him, beside the road, a dusty willow tree cast a speckled shade. Joad was soaked with sweat by the time he reached it. A man sat on the ground, leaning against the trunk of the tree. His legs were crossed. He did not hear Joad approaching, for he was solemnly whistling the tune of "Yes, Sir, That's My Baby." His foot swung slowly up and down in tempo. He stopped whistling and sang in an easy thin tenor.

Joad had moved into the imperfect shade of the willow tree before the man heard him coming. He stopped his song, and turned his head. It was a long head, bony; tight of skin, and set on a neck as stringy as a celery stalk. His eyeballs were heavy and stuck out. The lids stretched to cover them, and the lids were raw and red. His cheeks were brown and shiny and hairless and his mouth full. The nose, beaked and hard, stretched the skin so tightly that the bridge showed white. There was no sweat on the face, not even on the tall pale forehead. It was a very high forehead, lined with delicate blue veins at the temples. Fully half of the face was above the eyes. His stiff gray hair was mussed back from his brow as though he had combed it back with his fingers.

He wore overalls and a blue shirt. A denim coat with brass buttons and a creased, spotted brown hat lay on the ground beside him. Canvas sneakers, gray with dust, lay near where they had fallen when they were kicked off.

Joad stood in the speckled shade and said, "Hi. It's hotter'n hell on the road."

The man looked long at Joad. "Now ain't you young Tom Joad—old Tom's boy?"

"Yeah," said Joad. "Going home now."

"You wouldn't remember me, I guess," the man said. He smiled and his full lips revealed great horse teeth. "You was always too busy pulling little girls' pigtails when I give you the Holy Spirit. You maybe don't remember, but I do. You come to Jesus 'cause of the pigtail yanking. Baptized you in the irrigation.[1] Fighting and yelling like a cat."

Joad looked at him with drooped eyes. Then he laughed. "Why, you're the preacher what baptized me."

"I was a preacher," said the man seriously. "Reverend Jim Casy. Used to howl out the name of Jesus to glory. And used to get an irrigation ditch so full of sorry sinners half of 'em almost drowned. But not no more," he sighed. "Just Jim Casy now. Ain't got the call no more."

Joad said, "Sure, I remember you. You used to give a good meeting. I recollect one time you give a whole sermon walking around on your hands, yelling your head off. Ma liked you more than anybody. An' Granma says you was just full of the spirit." He dug at his rolled coat, found the right pocket, and pulled out a pint of whiskey. He unscrewed the cap and held out

---

1. **irrigation** ditch used for holding water for crops

the bottle. "Have a little snort?"

Casy took the bottle and looked at it broodingly. "I ain't preaching no more. The spirit ain't in the people much no more. Worse than that, the spirit ain't in me no more."

Joad mopped his face with his hat. "You ain't too damn holy to take a drink, are you?" he asked.

Casy seemed to see the bottle for the first time. He tilted it and took three big swallows. "Nice drinking liquor," he said.

"Ought to be," said Joad. "That's factory liquor. Cost a buck."

Casy took another swallow before he passed the bottle back. "Yes, sir!" he said. "Yes, sir!"

Joad took the bottle back from him, and in politeness did not wipe the neck with his sleeve before he drank. He squatted and set the bottle upright against his coat roll. His fingers found a twig, and used it to draw his thoughts on the ground. He swept the leaves from a square and smoothed the dust. And he drew angles and made little circles. "I ain't seen you in a long time," he said.

"Nobody's seen me," said the preacher. "I went off alone an' I sat and figured. The spirit's strong in me, only it ain't the same. I ain't so sure of a lot of things. Here I got the spirit sometimes an' nothing to preach about. I got the call to lead people, an' no place to lead them. And I'll tell you one more thing I figgered out."

"What did you figger?" asked Joad.

"I figgered about the Holy Spirit. I figgered, 'Why do we got to hang it on God or Jesus? Maybe,' I figgered, 'maybe it's all men an' all women we love; maybe that's the Holy Spirit—the human spirit. Maybe all men got one big soul that everybody's a part of.' Now I sat there thinking it, an' all of a sudden—I knew it. I knew it so deep down that it was true, and I still know it."

"You can't hold no church with ideas like that," Joad said.

"It's a funny thing," the preacher said. "I was thinking about ol' Tom Joad when you come along. Thinking I'd call in on him. How is Tom?"

"I don't know. I ain't been home in four years."

"Been out traveling around?" Casy asked.

"Might as well tell you now an' get it over with," Joad said. "But if you was still preaching I wouldn't tell, fear you get praying over me." He drained the last of the pint and flung it from him. The flat brown bottle skidded lightly over the dust. "I been in McAlester them four years."

Casy said, "Ain't wanting to talk about it, huh? I won't ask no questions, if you done something bad—"

"I'd do what I done—again," said Joad. "I killed a guy in a fight. We was drunk at a dance. He got a knife in me, an' I killed him with a shovel that was laying there. Knocked his head to squash."

"You ain't ashamed of nothing, then?"

"No," said Joad, "I ain't. Got seven years, since he had a knife in me. Got out in four—parole."

"Then you ain't heard nothing about your folks for four years?"

"Oh, I heard. Ma sent me a card two years ago, an' last Christmas Granma sent a card."

Joad and Casy talked about prison life for a while, until the sun sank lower. "Guess I'll mosey along," Joad said. "I hate to hit the sun but it ain't so bad now."

Casy pulled himself together. "I ain't seen ol' Tom in a long while," he said. "I was gonna look in on him anyways. I brought Jesus to your folks for a long time."

"Come along," Joad said. "Pa will be glad to see you." Tom picked up his coat roll and tightened it snugly about his shoes.

Casy slipped into his sneakers and said, "Ol' Tom's house can't be more than a mile from here. Ain't she over that third rise?"

"Sure," said Joad.

They hesitated on the edge of the shade and then plunged into the yellow sunlight like two swimmers hurrying to shore. After a few fast steps, they slowed to a gentle, thoughtful pace.

About a mile down the road, they moved over the curving top of the last rise and saw the Joad place below them. And Joad stopped. "It ain't the same," he said. "Look at that house. Something's happened. There ain't nobody there." The two stood and stared at the little cluster of buildings.

The owner men came onto the land. Some of the men were kind because they hated what they had to do. Some of them were angry because they hated to be cruel. And some of them were cold because they had long ago found that one could not be an owner unless one was cold. All of them were caught in something larger than themselves. The Bank or The Company must have, needs, wants, a profit.

At last the owner men came to the point. The tenant system[2] will not work anymore. One man on a tractor can take the place of 12 or 14 families. Pay him a wage and take all the crop. We don't like to do it, but we have to do it.

The tenants stood up angrily. Grampa killed

---

2. **tenant system** system in which a person farms land that another person owns. The tenant pays rent on that land, in cash or by giving the owner a portion of the crops that are raised.

Indians for the land, Pa killed snakes for the land. Then a bad year came and he had to borrow money. The bank owned the land then, but we stayed and got a little of what we raised. Even if it's no good, it's still ours. Being born on it, working it—that's what makes it ours. That's what makes ownership, not a paper with numbers on it.

And now the owner men grew angry. You'll have to go. You're on land that isn't yours.

But if we go, where'll we go? We got no money.

Why don't you go on west to California? There's work there, and it never gets cold. Why, you can reach out anywhere and pick an orange. Why, there's always some kind of crop to work in. Why don't you go there? And the owner men started their cars and rolled away.

The tenant men squatted down to mark the dust with a stick, to figure, to wonder.

The Reverend Casy and young Tom stood on the hill and looked down on the Joad place. The small unpainted house was mashed at one corner. It had been pushed off its foundations so that it slumped at an angle, its blind front windows pointing at a spot well above the horizon. The fences were gone and the cotton grew in the door and up against the house. The out-house lay on its side, and the cotton grew close about it.

"There ain't nobody living here." Tom said at last. They moved quickly down the hill. Tom looked into the barn shed. Deserted. Then he paused at the entrance to the tool shed. "There ain't nothing left. We had pretty nice tools. There ain't nothing left."

Casy said, "If I was still a preacher I'd say the arm of the Lord had struck. But now I don't know what happened. I been away. I didn't hear nothing."

Joad said, "Maybe they're all dead. But somebody'd have told me. I'd have got word some way."

"Let's look in the house," Casy said. "Maybe they left a letter or something. Would they have known you was coming out?"

"I don't know," said Joad. "No, I guess not. I didn't know myself till a week ago."

They found the house empty and deserted and went back outside. The preacher, staring off across the fields, said, "Look! Down there. Somebody's coming."

Joad squinted toward the fields. As the man drew closer, he said, "Why, we know him—that's Muley Graves." And he called, "Hey, Muley! How are ya?"

Muley Graves was a lean man, rather short. His movements were jerky and quick. His blue jeans were pale at the knee and seat. He wore an old black suit coat, stained and spotted, the sleeves torn loose from the shoulders in back, and ragged holes worn through at the elbows. His black hat was as stained as his coat, and the band, torn half free, flopped up and down as he walked. Muley's face was smooth and unwrinkled, but it wore the hateful look of a bad child. The mouth was held tight and small, the little eyes half scowling, half fretful.

"Who's that?" the advancing man called. Joad did not answer. Muley came close, very close, before he made out the faces. "Well, I'll be damned," he said. "It's Tommy Joad. When'd you get out, Tommy?"

"Two days ago," said Joad. "Took a little time to hitchhike home. An' look here what I find. Where's my folks, Muley? What's the house all smashed up for, an' cotton planted in the dooryard?"

"By God, it's lucky I come by!" said Muley. "'Cause ol' Tom worried that you might come home an' find everyone gone. When they was fixing to move I was setting in the kitchen there. I just told Tom I wasn't gonna move, so he asked me to keep an eye out for you if I was still around. I told him I'd be around. There ain't nobody can run a guy name of Graves out of this country. An' they ain't done it, neither."

Joad said impatiently, "Tell about you standing up to 'em later. Right now, where's my folks?"

"That's what I'm telling you. Took three trips with your Uncle John's wagon. Took the stove, an' the pump, an' the beds. You should a seen them beds go out, with all them kids an' your granma an' grampa setting up against the headboard." Joad opened his mouth to speak. "They're all at your Uncle John's," Muley said quickly.

"Oh! All at Uncle John's. Well, what they doing there? Now stick to the subject for a second, then you can go on your way. What they doing there?"

"Well, they been chopping cotton, all of 'em, even the kids an' your grampa. Getting money together so they can shove on west. Gonna buy a car and shove on west, where it's easy living."

Chapter 4

In the towns, in vacant lots, the used-car yards, the garages with signs—Used Cars, Good Used Cars. Checked Cars, Guaranteed Cars. Free Radio. Car With 100 Gallons of Gas Free. Come in and look. Used Cars.

A lot, and a house large enough for a desk and chair and a blue book. Sheaf of contracts, dog-eared, held with paper clips, and a neat pile of unused contracts. Pen—keep it full. A sale's been lost 'cause a pen didn't work.

Owners with rolled-up sleeves. Salesmen, neat, deadly, small eyes watching for weaknesses. Over there, them two people—no, with the kids. Get 'em in a car. Going to California? Here's just what you need. Looks shot, but they's thousand's of miles still in her. Get 'em rolling. Get 'em out in a jalopy. Sock it to 'em!

Flags, red and white, white and blue—all along the curb. Used Cars. Good Cars.

The sky grayed among the stars. Tom Joad and the preacher walked quickly along a road that was only wheel tracks through a cotton field. The two men walked in silence and smelled the dust their feet kicked into the air.

A redness grew up out of the eastern horizon. On the ground birds began to chirp, sharply. "Look!" said Joad. "Right ahead. That's Uncle John's tank. Can't see the windmill, but there's his tank. See it against the sky?" He speeded his walk. "I wonder if all the folks are there."

They saw the tank legs now, and the house, a square little box, unpainted and bare, and the low-

roofed barn. In the yard was piled furniture, the
blades and motor of the windmill, bedsteads, chairs,
tables. "My God, they're fixing to go!" Joad said.

A strange-looking truck stood in the yard. It was a
Hudson Super-Six sedan,[1] but the top had been ripped
in two with a chisel, and the top had been cut off in the
middle and the truck bed fitted on. Old Tom Joad stood
in the truck bed and was nailing on the top rails of the
truck sides. His grizzled, bearded face was low over
his work, and a bunch of nails stuck out of his mouth.
He set a nail and hammered it in.

Young Tom came forward toward the truck. He wet
his thick lips with his tongue, and he said softly, "Pa."

"What do you want?" old Tom mumbled around a
mouthful of nails. He wore a black, dirty slouch hat
and a blue work shirt over which was a buttonless
vest. His jeans were held up by a wide leather belt
with a big square brass buckle. The sleeves of his shirt
were tight on his forearms, held down by the bulging,
powerful muscles. Stomach and hips were lean, and
legs short, heavy, and strong. His eyes were brown,
black-coffee brown, and he thrust his head forward
when he looked at a thing, for his bright dark eyes
were failing. He held his hammer in the air and looked
over the truck side at Tom. And he said wonderingly,
as though he told himself the fact, "It's Tommy—it's
Tommy come home."

His mouth opened again and a look of fear came
into his eyes. "Tommy," he said softly, "you ain't busted
out? You ain't got to hide?" He listened tensely.

"Naw," said Tom. "I'm paroled. I'm free."

Old Tom laid his hammer down and dropped to the
ground. "Tommy," he said, "we're going to California.

---

1. **sedan** car that holds four to seven passengers

But we was gonna write you a letter an' tell you." And he said, almost not believing it. "But you're back. You can go with us. You can go!" He looked at Jim Casy.

Tom said, "You remember the preacher, Pa. He come along with me."

"He been in prison too?"

"No, I met him on the road. He been away."

Pa shook hands gravely. "You're welcome here, sir."

Casy said, "Glad to be here. It's a thing to see when a boy comes home. It's a thing to see."

"Home," Pa said.

"To his folks," the preacher said quickly. "We stayed at the other place last night."

"Let's surprise your ma," Pa said. His face was alive with excitement. He went on into the house and Tom heard him say, "Ma, there's a couple of fellows just come along the road. They wonder if we could spare a bite."

"Let 'em come," she said in a cool, calm drawl, friendly and humble. "We got plenty. The bread is done, an' I'm just taking up the sidemeat now."

Tom stood looking in. Ma was heavy, but not fat; thick with child-bearing and work. She wore a loose Mother Hubbard[2] of gray cloth with a wash-faded flower pattern. Her thin, steel-gray hair was gathered in a sparse wispy knot at the back of her head. Strong, freckled arms were bare to the elbow. Her hands were chubby and delicate, like those of a plump little girl. She looked out into the sunshine. Her full face was not soft; it was controlled, kindly.

Her hazel eyes seemed to have experienced all possible tragedy and to have climbed pain and suffering as if they were steps into a higher calm and superhu-

---

2. Mother Hubbard loose dress

man understanding. She seemed to know, to accept, and to welcome her position. She seemed to understand that if she swayed, the family shook, and if she ever deeply wavered or despaired, the family would fall.

She looked up pleasantly from the frying pan. Her eyes opened wide. Then her hand sank slowly to her side and the fork clattered to the wooden floor. She breathed heavily, then closed her eyes. "Thank God," she said. "Oh, thank God!" And suddenly her face was worried. "Tommy, you ain't wanted? You didn't bust loose?"

"No, Ma. Parole. I got the papers in my pocket."

Her fingers went to his cheek as a blind man's fingers might. And her joy was nearly like sorrow. She struggled to control herself. Her breath came out explosively. "Well!" she cried. "We come mighty near to going without you. An' we was wondering how in the world you could ever find us." She picked up the fork and stirred some pork strips, curling and sizzling in the frying pan.

Old Tom giggled, "Fooled you, huh, Ma? Wished Grampa'd been here to see. Looked like somebody had beat ya between the eyes with a sledge."

Tom asked, "Where is Grampa? I ain't seen the old devil."

"Oh, him an' Granma sleeps in the barn. They got to get up so much in the night. They was stumbling over the little fellas."

Ma said, "Pa, run out an' tell them Tommy's home. Grampa's a favorite of his."

"Of course," said Pa. "I should of done it before."

Tom watched him go while his mother poured coffee. She did not look at him. "Tommy," she said hesitantly, timidly, "I got to ask you—you ain't mad?"

"Mad, Ma?"

"You ain't mad? You don't hate nobody? They didn't do nothing in that jail to rot you out with crazy mad?"

"No-o-o," he said. "I was for a little while, but I let stuff run off me. I ain't mad."

She sighed, "Thank God!" under her breath.

Across the yard came four people. Grampa was ahead, a lean, ragged, quick old man, jumping with quick steps and favoring his right leg. He wore dark ragged pants and a torn blue shirt, open all the way down, and showing long gray underwear. His lean face was complaining, mischievous, and laughing. He fought and argued, told dirty stories. He drank too much when he could get it, ate too much when it was there, talked too much all the time.

Behind him hobbled Granma, who had survived only because she was as mean as her husband. She had held her own with a fierce religious feeling that was as savage as anything Grampa could offer. As she walked she hiked her Mother Hubbard up to her knees, and she bleated her shrill terrible war cry: "Pu-raise Gawd for victory!"

Granma and Grampa raced each other to get across the broad yard. They fought over everything, and loved and needed the fighting.

Behind them, moving slowly and evenly, but keeping up, came Pa and Noah—Noah the first-born, tall and strange, walking always with a wondering look on his face, calm and puzzled. He was not stupid but he was strange. Pa thought he knew why Noah was strange, but Pa was ashamed and never told. Frightened at the birth, Pa had pulled and twisted the baby to get it out. The midwife, arriving late, had found the baby's neck stretched and its body warped. She had pushed the head back and molded the body with her hands. But Pa always remembered, and was ashamed. He was kinder to Noah than to the others.

Grampa walked up and slapped Tom on the chest, and his eyes grinned with pride. "How are ya, Tommy?"

"OK," said Tom. "How ya keeping yourself?"

"Full of vice and vinegar," said Grampa.

Tom grinned and said, "Ain't he a heller?"

Granma beamed. "A wickeder man never lived. He's going to hell on a poker, praise Gawd! Wants to drive the truck!" she said spitefully. "Well, he ain't going to."

Noah stood on the step. He faced Tom, and his wide-set eyes seemed to look around him. His face had little expression. Tom said, "How are ya, Noah?"

"Fine," said Noah. "How're you?" That was all, but it was a comfortable thing.

Ma called the family to eat. Suddenly Tom said, "Hey. Where's the preacher?"

Granma raised a shrill voice, "Preacher? You got a preacher? Go get him. We'll have a grace."

Tom stepped out on the porch. "Hey, Jim! Jim Casy!" he called. The preacher came out from under the tank. Tom asked, "What was you doing, hiding?"

"Well, no. But a fellow shouldn't butt his head in where a family got family stuff."

"Come on in an' eat," said Tom. "Granma wants a grace."

"But I ain't a preacher no more," protested Casy.

"Aw, come on. Give her a grace. Don't do you no harm, an' she likes 'em." They walked inside together.

After eating, the men went out and stood around the truck. Tom opened the hood and looked at the big greasy engine. Pa said, "Your brother Al looked her over before we bought her. He says she's all right."

"What's he know? He's just a squirt," said Tom.

"He worked driving a truck last year. Smart aleck like he is, he knows quite a bit. He can tinker an engine, Al can."

Tom asked, "Where's he now?"

"Well," said Pa, "he's going around the country. He don't think of nothing but girls and engines. A plain smart aleck. Ain't been in for a week."

"Where's Uncle John?" Tom asked. "Where's Rose of Sharon? Where's Ruthie an' Winfield? Nobody said nothing about them yet."

Pa said, "Nobody asked. John gone to Sallisaw with the horse and wagon and a load of stuff to sell: pump, tools, chickens. Took Ruthie and Winfield with him. Went before daylight."

"Funny I never saw him," said Tom.

"Well, you come down from the highway, didn't you? He took the back way. An' Rosasharn, she's with Connie's folks. By God! You don't even know! Rosasharn's married to Connie Rivers. You remember Connie. Nice young fellow. An' Rosasharn's due about three–four–five months now. Looks fine."

"Geez!" said Tom. "Rosasharn was just a little kid. An' now she's gonna have a baby. So darn much happens in four years if you're away. When ya thinkin' to start out west, Pa?"

"Well, we got to take this stuff in the yard and sell it. If Al gets back, I figgered he could load the truck an' take all of it in, an' maybe we could start out tomorrow or day after. We ain't got much money, an' it's darn near 2,000 miles to California. Quicker we get started, surer it is we get there. Money's a-dribbling out all the time. You got any money?"

"Only a couple of dollars. How'd you get money?"

"We sold all the stuff at our place," said Pa, "an' the whole bunch of us chopped cotton, even Grampa. We put everything together—200 dollars. We give 75 for this here truck, an' me an' Al cut her in two an' built on this here back. Darn ol' tires on this truck ain't gonna go far. Got a couple of wore out spares. Pick up stuff along the road, I guess." Pa stared down the road. "If I ain't mistaken, there's a young smart aleck dragging his tail home right now. Looks wore out, too."

Al wore a Stetson hat at an angle and stiff jeans with the bottoms turned up eight inches to show his heeled boots. He walked close before he recognized Tom. The two brothers shook hands. And there was a liking between these two.

Tom said, "Hello. Geez, you're growing like a bean. I wouldn't have known you."

Pa said to Al, "You look wore out. Well, you got to take a load into Sallisaw to sell."

Al had inspired some admiration among boys of his own age because his brother had killed a man. He looked at Tom. "Care to ride in?" he said as casually as he could.

"No, I can't," said Tom. "I'll help around here. We'll be—together on the road."

Al had to ask. "Did—did you bust out? Of jail?"

"No," said Tom. "I got paroled."

"Oh." And Al was a little disappointed.

In the little houses, the tenant people sifted their belongings and the belongings of their fathers and of their grandfathers. They picked over their possessions for the journey west. The men were ruthless because the past had been spoiled, but the women knew how the past would cry to them in the coming days. How will we know it is us without our past? No. Leave it. Burn it.

They piled up the goods in the yard—goods they

could not sell, or carry to far-off California—and set fire to them. They stood and watched them burning, and then frantically they loaded up the cars and drove away, drove in the dust. The dust hung in the air for a long time after the loaded cars had passed.

After Al left for Sallisaw with a load of the Joads' goods to sell, Ma said to Tom, "I hope things is all right in California."

"What makes you think they ain't?"

"Well—nothing. Seems too nice, kinda. I seen the handbills[3] fellas pass out, an' how much work they is, an' high wages an' all. I seen in the paper how they want folks to come an' pick grapes an' oranges an' peaches. That'd be nice work, Tom. But I'm scared of stuff so nice. I ain't got faith. I'm scared something ain't so nice about it. But I like to think how nice it's gonna be, maybe, in California."

The preacher joined Ma and Tom on the doorstep. "I got to get going west," he said. "I got to go. I wonder if I can go along with you folks."

Ma waited for Tom to answer, but he kept silent. So Ma said, "Pa says all the men'll talk tonight and figger when we gonna start. I guess we better not say until all the men come. John, an' Pa, an' Noah, an' Tom, an' Grampa, an' Al, an' Connie, they're gonna figger as soon as they get back. But if there's room, I'm pretty sure we'll be proud to have you."

The preacher sighed. "I'll go anyways," he said. "Something's happening. I went up an' I looked, an' the houses are all empty, an' the land is empty, an' this whole country is empty. I can't stay here no more.

---

3. **handbill**   small printed sheet of advertising passed out by hand

I got to go where the folks is going."

In the late afternoon the truck came back. Al sat bent over the wheel, proud and serious, and Pa and Uncle John, as heads of the family, had the honor seats beside the driver.

Standing in the truck bed, holding onto the bars of the sides, rode the others. There was 12-year-old Ruthie and 10-year-old Winfield, grime-faced and wild, the edges of their mouths black and sticky from licorice sticks, coaxed out of their father in town.

Beside them, clinging lightly to the bars, stood Rose of Sharon. She balanced, swaying on the balls of her feet, and took up the road shock in her knees, for Rose of Sharon was pregnant and careful. Her round soft face, which had been inviting only a few months ago, had already put on the barrier of pregnancy. Her whole body had become serious. Her whole thought and action were directed inward on the baby.

Connie, her 19-year-old husband, who had married a plump, passionate hoyden,[4] was still frightened and bewildered at the change in her. This was a careful, wise creature who smiled shyly but firmly at him. Connie was proud and fearful of Rose of Sharon. Whenever he could, he put a hand on her or stood close, so that his body touched her at hip and shoulder, and he felt that this kept a relation that might be departing.

Connie was a sharp-faced, lean young man of Texas, and his pale blue eyes were sometimes dangerous and sometimes kindly, and sometimes frightened. He drank enough, but not too much; fought when it was needed; and never boasted. He was a good hard worker when he wanted to be. Most of the time, he seemed to

---

4. **hoyden**   carefree girl or woman; a flirt

make a good husband.

Had he not been 50 years old, and so one of the natural rulers of the family, Uncle John would have preferred not to sit in the honor place beside the driver. He would have liked Rose of Sharon to sit there. This was impossible because she was young and a woman. Still, Uncle John, a lonely man and a loner since the death of his wife, sat uneasily. Being one of the heads of the family, he had to govern; and now he had to sit on the honor seat beside the driver.

The family gathered later in the softening evening light, for a while sitting or standing in silence. Then Pa made his report. "Got skinned on the stuff we sold. The fella knowed we couldn't wait. Got 18 dollars only."

Noah, the oldest son, asked, "How much, all added up, we got?"

"Hundred fifty-four," Pa said. "Means we got to figger close. It's a sad thing to figger close. Let's see now. There's Grampa an' Granma—that's 2. An' me an' John an' Ma—that's 5. An' Noah an' Tommy an' Al— that's 8. Rosasharn an' Connie is 10, an' Ruthie an' Winfiel' is 12. We got to take the dogs 'cause we can't shoot a good dog, an' there ain't nobody to give them to. An' that's 14."

"Not counting what chickens is left, an' two pigs," said Noah.

Pa said, "I aim to get them pigs salted down to eat on the way. We gonna need meat. Carry the salt kegs right with us. But I'm wondering if we can all ride and the preacher too. An' can we feed an extra mouth?" Without turning his head he asked, "Can we, Ma?"

Ma cleared her throat. "It ain't can we. It's will we." she said firmly. "An' the answer is yes."

Uncle John broke in. "What we hanging around for? Now we're going, why don't we go?"

The whole family worked through the night, butchering and packing the pigs, loading the truck with all that it could haul, and yanking up the roots of three generations of Joads.

The first gray of daylight began in the sky, and the work was done—the kegs of pork ready, the truck loaded, and the chicken coop ready to go on top. Suddenly, the dogs began barking. A man was approaching. It was Muley Graves, his hat pulled low. "I was just walking around, an' I thought I'd maybe say good-by."

Pa said, "You almost missed us. We're ready to go."

Noah said, "How about the dogs, Pa?"

"I forgot the dogs," Pa said. He threw one on top of the heap where Noah caught him. "Got to leave the other two."

Muley said, "I'd like to have a couple of dogs. I'll take 'em." The last tie was severed.

Al got in the driver's seat. The starter whirred and caught. The truck shuddered and strained across the yard. Ma tried to look back, but the load cut off her view. She straightened her head. A great weariness was in her eyes. And the truck crawled slowly through the dust, toward the highway and the west.

Chapter 5

The houses were left vacant on the land, and the land was vacant because of this. Only the tractor sheds, silver and gleaming, were alive. They were alive with metal and gasoline and oil, the disks of the plows shining. The tractors had lights shining, for there is no day and night for a tractor. The disks turn the earth in the darkness and in the daylight. The work is easy and efficient. So easy that the wonder goes out of the work, so efficient that the wonder goes out of the land and the working of it. When the wonder is gone, so is the deep understanding and the relation. When the iron doors of the tractor shed are shut, the tractor man goes home, and his home is not the land.

Highway 66 is the main migrant[1] road. Sixty-six—the long concrete path across the country. Over the red lands and the gray lands, twisting up into the mountains. It crosses the Divide[2] and moves down into the bright and terrible desert, and across the desert into the mountains again, and into the rich California valleys. Highway 66 is the path of people in flight.

Two hundred and fifty thousand people pass over the road. Fifty thousand old cars—wounded, steaming. Wrecks along the road, abandoned. Well, what happened to the folks in that car? Did they walk? Where are they? Where does the courage come from?

---

1. **migrant** person who moves from place to place to find work harvesting crops
2. **Divide** the Continental or Great Divide; the main ridge of the Rocky Mountains

Where does the terrible faith come from?

The people in flight from the terror behind—
strange things happen to them. Some things are bit-
terly cruel and some are so beautiful that faith is
restored forever.

The ancient overloaded Hudson creaked and grunt-
ed to the highway at Sallisaw and turned west, and
the sun was blinding. But on the concrete road Al built
up his speed because the flattened springs were not in
danger anymore. The sun was overhead when they
reached Castle, 101 miles down the road.

Al shifted himself on the broken seat and changed
his grip on the steering wheel. And he sighed, "Makes
a racket, but I think she's all right. God knows what
she'll do if we got to climb with the load we got. Got
any hills between here and California, Ma?"

"Seems to me there's hills," she said. "'Course I don't
know. But seems to me I heard there's hills an' even
mountains. Big ones."

Granma, asleep, drew a long whining sigh.

Al said, "We'll burn right up if we got climbing to do.
Have to throw out some of this stuff. Maybe we
shouldn't have brought that preacher."

"You'll be glad of that preacher before we're
through," said Ma. "That preacher'll help us."

"Ma—" Al began with difficulty, then began again.
"Ma, you scared going to a new place?"

"A little," she said. "Only it ain't like scared so
much. I'm just setting here, waiting. When something
happens that I got to do something—I'll do it."

"Ain't you thinking what it's gonna be like when we
get there? Ain't you scared it won't be nice like we
thought?"

"No," she said quickly. "No I ain't. You can't do that.

I can't do that. It's too much—living too many lives. Up ahead there's 1,000 lives we might live, but when it comes, it'll only be one."

Out of Castle, Al pulled off the highway so that Granma could take care of some business behind the roadside bushes. On top of the truck, the others stirred to life; all except Grampa who felt poorly, and wouldn't move. The rest let themselves down to stretch their legs and gnaw the pork bones.

Pa said, "Where's the water?"

"Ain't it with you?" Ma asked. "I set out that gallon jug."

Pa climbed the sides and looked under the canvas. "It ain't here. We must have forgot it."

Thirst, and a little panic, seized them all instantly. Al felt the fear growing. "We'll get water at the first service station we come to. We need gas, too."

Castle to Paden—25 miles and the sun started down. Near Paden there was a shack beside the road and two gas tanks in front of it. Beside a fence, a water faucet and a hose. Al drove in and nosed the Hudson up to the hose. A stout man with a scowl on his red face greeted them.

"You folks aim to buy anything?" he asked.

Al said, "Need some gas, mister."

"Got any money?"

"Sure. Think we're begging?"

The scowl left the fat man's face. "Well, that's all right, folks. Help yourself to the water." And he hastened to explain. "Road is full of people, come in, use water, dirty up the toilet, an' then, by God, they'll steal stuff an' don't buy nothing. Got no money to buy with. Come begging a gallon of gas to move on."

Tom dropped angrily to the ground and moved toward the fat man. "We're paying our way," he said fiercely. "You got no call to give us a going-over. We ain't asked you for nothing."

"I ain't," the fat man said quickly. "Just help yourself to water, and go use the toilet if you want."

The Joads' dog sniffed his way among the dusty weeds beside the road, to the edge of the pavement. He raised his head and looked across, and then started over. Rose of Sharon screamed shrilly. A big car whisked near, tires squealed. The dog dodged helplessly, and with a shriek went under the wheels. The big car slowed for a moment and faces looked back, and then it gathered greater speed and disappeared. And the dog, a blot of blood and tangled, burst intestines, kicked slowly in the road.

Uncle John said, "I ought to have tied him up."

Pa looked down at the dog for a moment and then he turned away. "Just as well, maybe," he said. "I don't know how we was gonna feed him anyways."

The fat man said, "Don't you folks worry none about it. I'll bury him out in the corn field."

Ruthie and Winfield looked at the dog before climbing back on the truck. Ruthie whispered, "His eyes was still open."

Winfield said boldly, "His guts was just all over—all over." After a moment's silence, he rolled over quickly and vomited down the side of the truck. When he sat up again his eyes were watery and his nose was running. "It ain't like killing pigs," he said in explanation.

Paden to Meeker, 13 miles; Meeker to Harrah, 14 miles; then on to Oklahoma City—the big city. Tom was at the wheel now. Oklahoma City to Bethany, another 14 miles.

Ma had been silent for a long time. "Tom, your Pa told me about you crossing the state line—"

Tom was a long time answering. "What about it, Ma?"

"Minute you cross the line you done a crime."

"Well, that's better than sticking around Sallisaw an' starving to death," he said. "We better look out for a place to stop for the night."

On the far side of Bethany, Tom pulled off the road where a touring car was parked. A little tent was pitched beside it. The hood of the old car was up, and a lean, middle-aged man stood looking down at the motor. His eyes were puzzled and angry. Tom leaned out the window. "Any law against folks stopping here for the night?"

The man introduced himself as Ivy Wilson, from Gelena, Kansas, and said, "I don't know. We only stopped here because we couldn't get no further. But you're welcome to share the space." And he called, "Sairy, there's some folks going to stay with us. Come on out an' say how do you do." Then he added, "Sairy ain't well."

The tent flaps opened and a small woman came out. Sairy was a skeleton covered with wrinkled skin. She held herself upright by a tent flap. "Tell them welcome," she said. "Tell them good an' welcome."

Noah and Uncle John and the preacher began to unload the truck. They helped Grampa down and sat him on the ground and he sat limply, staring ahead of him. "You sick, Grampa?" Noah asked.

"Sicker'n hell," said Grampa weakly. Without warning, he began to cry. At Sairy's bidding, they carried him into the tent.

Uncle John said, "He must be good an' sick. Ain't never seen him blubbering in my life."

Ma went over to Casy and said, "You been around sick people a lot. Won't you go take a look at him?"

Casy looked at Grampa and said, "I think—maybe—he's working up a stroke."

Ma looked through the flaps. "Granma wants to come in. Should she?"

The preacher said, "She'll just fret if she don't."

"Think he's all right?" Ma asked.

Casy shook his head slowly. Ma looked down at the struggling old face with blood pounding through it. She drew outside and her voice came through. "He's all right, Granma. He's just taking a little rest."

And Granma answered sulkily, "Well, I want to see him. He's a tricky devil. He wouldn't never let ya know." She entered the tent and looked at Grampa. "He's sulking," she said. "I told you he was tricky."

Casy said gently, "He ain't sulking, he's sick."

"Oh!" She looked down at the old man again. "Sick bad, you think?"

"Purty bad, Granma."

"Then why ain't you prayin'?"

"I told you, Granma, I ain't a preacher."

"Pray, I tell ya," Granma cried. "Pray, damn you!"

Casy looked at her for a moment. Grampa's breath rasped and became louder, more uneven. "Our Father which are in Heaven, hallowed be Thy Name—"

"Hallelujah!" said Granma.

A long gasping sigh came from Grampa's open mouth, and then a crying release of air.

"Amen," said Casy.

Sairy took Granma by the arm and led her outside, and Granma moved with dignity and held her head high.

Casy looked down into Grampa's eyes and they were clear and deep, and there was a knowing, calm look in them.

"What was it?" Pa asked softly.

"Stroke," said Casy. "A good quick stroke."

They buried Grampa six feet deep at the bottom of a

gulch. With him, they buried a note in a bottle, written by Tom. In big clear letters, the note said: "This here is William James Joad, dyed of a stroke. His fokes bured him becaws they got no money to pay for funerls. Nobody kilt him. Jus a stroke and he dyed."

Suddenly, Al got up and walked to the Wilsons' car. He looked at it for a moment and then came back and sat down. Tom watched his younger brother carefully. "I was thinking like that myself," he said. "We got an overload, but Mr. and Mrs. Wilson ain't. If some of us folks could ride with them, we could get up hills. And me and Al both knows about a car, so we could keep that car rolling. We'd keep together on the road, and it'd be good for everybody."

Wilson jumped up. "Why, sure. We'd be proud. Wouldn't we, Sairy?"

"Wouldn't be a burden on you folks?" said Sairy.

"No, by God," said Pa. "You'd be helping us."

Sairy said, "If I get sick again, you got to go on."

Ma looked carefully at Sairy and seemed to see for the first time the face that was shrinking with pain. And Ma said, "We gonna see you through."

Along Highway 66 the hamburger stands—Al & Susy's Place—Carl's Lunch—Joe & Minnie—Will's Eats. Two gasoline pumps in front, a screen door, a long bar, stools, and a foot rail. The walls decorated with posters of bathing girls and advertisements for No-Doze, Bromo-Seltzer, Alka-Seltzer, Coca Cola. And always a jukebox with records by Bing Crosby and Benny Goodman.

Minnie or Susy or Mae, middle-aging behind the counter, hair curled and rouge and powder on a sweating face. Taking orders in a soft low voice, calling them to the cook with a screech like a peacock.

Cars whisking by on Highway 66. License plates. Mass., Tenn., R.I., Vt., Ohio. Going west. Fine cars, cruising at 65.

Mae says to Big Bill the trucker, "There was a Massachusetts car stopped a while ago."

Big Bill says, "You ought to be out on 66. Cars from all over the country. All heading west. Never seen so many before."

Mae says, "I hope none of them darn vagrants[3] comes begging by here today."

Steam spurts from the valve of the coffee urn. The ice machine chugs softly for a while and then stops. The electric fan in the corner waves its head slowly back and forth, sweeping the room with a warm breeze. On the highway, on 66, the cars whiz by.

Al cleaned out the clogged fuel line on the Wilsons' touring car, and the Joads and Wilsons crawled westward as a unit. El Reno and Bridgeport, Clinton, Elk City, Sayre, and Texola. There's the border, and Oklahoma was behind. And this day the cars crawled on and on, through the panhandle of Texas. They went through Amarillo in the evening, drove too long, and camped when it was dusk. Granma had convulsions from the heat, and she was weak when they stopped.

Two days, the families were in flight out of Oklahoma and across Texas. But on the third day the land became too huge for them and they settled into a new way of living. The highway became their home and movement their medium of expression. Little by little, they settled into the new life. Wildorado and Vega and Boise and Glenrio. New Mexico and the

---

3. **vagrant** homeless person

mountains. In the far distance, waved up against the sky, the mountains stood. And the wheels of the cars creaked around, and the engines were hot. They crawled to the Pecos river, and crossed at Santa Rosa. And they went on for 20 miles.

Al Joad drove the touring car, and his mother and Rose of Sharon sat beside him. Suddenly Al grew tense over the wheel. A little rattle had developed in the engine. He speeded up and the rattle increased. Al blew his horn and pulled the car to the side of the road. Ahead, the truck pulled up and then backed slowly. Tom got out and walked to the touring car. "What's the matter, Al?"

Al speeded the motor. "Listen to her." The rattling was louder now. "Con-rod[4] bearing, ain't it?"

"Sounds like it," Tom said.

Wilson asked, "Is it bad?"

"Pretty bad," said Tom. He left to tell the others.

Ma asked Al, "Is it terrible bad?"

"Well, it's hard to get at, an' we got to get a new con-rod or else some babbitt[5] in this one," Al said. "Sure am glad Tom's here. I never fitted no bearing. Hope to God Tom did."

Tom said, "Good day's job. Got to go back to that last place for a part, Santa Rosa. Albuquerque's about 75 miles on. Me and Casy will stop here and fix this car. You drive on. We'll catch up with you."

Pa said, "Well, if that's the way it's gonna go, we'd better get moving. We can maybe squeeze in 100 miles before we stop."

"I ain't gonna go," said Ma.

---

4. con-rod connecting rod that transmits power from one part of an engine to another
5. babbitt a metal lining

"What you mean?" Pa was amazed at the revolt.

Ma stepped to the car and picked up a jack handle. "I ain't gonna go. Only way you gonna get me is to whip me."

"Ma, what's eating on you?" Tom asked. "What's the matter with you, anyways?"

Ma's face softened, but her eyes were fierce. "What we got left in the world? Nothing but us. And now, right off, you want to bust up the folks—" Ma had taken control.

Tom said soothingly, "Ma, we can't all camp here. Granma needs shade."

"All right," said Ma. "We'll stop first place there's shade. And the truck will come back and take you in town to get your part, and it'll bring you back."

Tom and Casy fixed the car and found the family at a campground down the road. Pa came to the gate. "Thought you was gonna be all week. Get her fixed?"

"We was pig lucky," said Tom. "Got a part before dark. We can get going first thing in the morning."

"That's a pretty nice thing," said Pa. "Ma's worried. Your Granma's taken poorly. She's sleeping now."

A small wooden house belonging to the owner dominated the campground. On the porch of the house a gasoline lantern hissed and threw its white glare in a great circle. The owner, a sullen lanky man, sat leaning back against the wall in a chair on the porch. A gathering of men surrounded him.

The owner dropped his front chair legs to the floor and said, "If you want to pull in here and camp it'll cost you four bits."

Tom said, "We can sleep in the ditch right beside the road, an' it won't cost nothing."

The owner said, "Deputy sheriff comes on by in the night. Might make it tough for ya. Got a law about sleeping out in this state. Got a law about vagrants."

"If I pay you 50 cents I ain't a vagrant, huh?"

"That's right."

Tom's eyes glowed angrily. "Deputy sheriff ain't your brother-in-law by any chance?"

The owner leaned forward. "No, he ain't. An' the time ain't come yet when us local folks got to take no talk from you damn bums, neither."

"It don't trouble you none to take our four bits. An' when did we get to be bums? We ain't asked ya for nothing. All of us bums, huh? Well, we ain't asking no nickels from you for the chance to lay down and rest."

In one of the tents a child cried, and a woman's soft voice soothed it and then broke into a low song, "Jesus loves you in the night. Sleep good, sleep good. Jesus watches in the night. Sleep, oh, sleep, oh."

Pa said, "Look, mister. We paid. This here fellow is part of our folks. Can't he stay? We paid."

"Half a dollar a car," said the owner.

Tom said, "We'll drive along the road. We'll watch for ya. Al can stay an' Uncle John can come with us—" He looked at the owner. "That all right with you?"

"If the same number stays that come an' paid—that's all right."

"We'll go along pretty soon," Tom said.

Then Pa spoke to the circle of men. "It's dirt hard for folks to tear up an' go. Folks like us that had our place. We ain't shiftless. We was people with a farm."

A thin young man turned his head. "Cropping?"

"Sure, we was sharecropping. Used to own the place."

"Same as us," the young man said.

"Lucky for us it ain't gonna last long," said Pa. "We'll get out west an' we'll get work an' we'll get a piece of growing land with water."

A ragged man stood near the edge of the porch. "You folks all going to California, I bet."

"That's right."

The ragged man said slowly, "Me—I'm coming back. I been there. There ain't no work out there."

Pa said, "What the hell you talking about? I got a handbill says they got good wages, an' a little while ago I seen a thing in the paper says they need folks to pick fruit. Don't make no sense if they don't need men. Cost money to put out them damn handbills."

"Look," said the man. "This fellow wants 800 men. So he prints up 5,000 of them things and maybe 20,000 people sees them. And maybe 2,000 folks get moving, folks that's crazy with worry."

"But it don't make no sense!" Pa cried.

"He needs maybe 200 men. When they get to the place, there's 1,000 men. The fellow says, 'I'm paying 20 cents an hour,' and maybe half the men walk off, but there's still 500 so hungry they'll work for nothing but biscuits."

The circle of faces looked coldly at him. The eyes tested his words. Finally, the ragged man said, "I tried to tell you folks something it took me a year to find out. Took two kids dead, took my wife dead to show me. But I can't tell you. Nobody couldn't tell me, neither. I can't tell you about them little fellows laying in the tent with their bellies puffed out and just skin on their bones."

The Joad men moved away. Pa said, "Suppose he's telling the truth—that fellow?"

The preacher answered. "He's telling the truth for him, all right. He wasn't making nothing up."

"Is that the truth for us?" Tom demanded.

"I don't know," said Pa.

"I don't know," said Casy.

In the evening, a strange thing happened. The 20 families became one family. The children were the children of all. Every night a world created, and every morning the world torn down like a circus.

The families learned what rights must be observed. The right of privacy in the tent. The right to keep the past hidden in the heart. The right to talk and to listen. And as the worlds moved westward, rules became laws, although no one told the families. It is unlawful to foul the drinking water. It is unlawful to eat good rich food near one who is hungry.

And with the laws, the punishments. There were only two: a quick fight or isolation. Isolation was the worst. For if one broke the laws, his name and face went with him, and he had no place in any world.

There grew up government in the worlds, with leaders. A man who was wise found that his wisdom was needed in every camp. A kind of insurance developed. A man with food fed a hungry man, and insured himself against hunger. And when a baby died, a pile of silver coins grew at the tent flap, for a baby must be well buried, since it had nothing else of life. An old man may be left in a poor grave, but not a baby.

Every night passed, and with the dawn the women came out of the tents, built the fires, put the coffee to boil. And the men came out and talked softly in the dawn. When you cross the Colorado River, there's the desert. Look out for the desert. Take plenty of water.

The families ate quickly, and the dishes were dipped and wiped. There was a rush to go. And when the sun rose, the camping place was vacant. And the camping place was ready for a new world in a new night.

Along the highway the cars of the migrant people crawled out like bugs, and the narrow concrete miles stretched ahead.

Chapter 6

The Joad family moved slowly westward, up into the mountains of New Mexico. They climbed into the high country of Arizona, and through a gap they looked down on the Painted Desert. A border guard stopped them.

"Where you going?"

"To California," said Tom.

"How long you plan to be in Arizona?"

"No longer than we can get across her."

"Got any plants?"

"No."

The guard put a little sticker on the windshield. "OK. Go ahead, but you better keep moving."

They crawled up the slopes, and the low twisted trees covered the slopes. The sun drained the dry rocky country, and ahead were jagged broken peaks, the western wall of Arizona. And now they were in a flight from the sun and the drought.

They drove all night, and came to the mountains. They crawled up the summit in the dark and came slowly down in the late night. When the daylight came they saw the Colorado river below them.

They drove to Topock, where a guard washed off the windshield sticker. Then into the broken rock wilderness. And although they were dead weary and the morning heat was growing, they stopped.

Pa called, "We're there—we're in California!" They looked dully at the broken rock glaring under the sun.

"We got the desert," said Tom. "We got to get to the water and rest."

The road runs parallel to the river, and it was well

into the morning when the burning motors came to Needles, where the river runs swiftly in the reeds.

There was a little camp by the river, 11 tents near the water. The two cars pulled to a clear place on the swamp grass, and the Joads and Wilsons set up a tent and stretched a tarpaulin[1] over a rope. Tom said, "I'm gonna go down an' take a bath before I sleep. How's Granma since we got her in the tent?"

"Don't know," said Pa. "Couldn't seem to wake her up." He cocked his head toward the tent. A whining bubbling voice came from under the canvas. Ma went quickly inside.

"She woke up, all right," said Noah. "She's all out of sense."

Tom said, "Hell, she's wore out. If she don't get some rest pretty soon, she ain't gonna last. She's just wore out. Anybody coming with me? I'm gonna wash, an' I'm gonna sleep in the shade—all day long." The men walked to the water and sat soaking themselves, looking across at the sharp peaks called Needles, and at the white rock mountains of Arizona.

Uncle John said, "This here's California, and she don't look so prosperous."

"Got the desert yet," said Tom. "An' I hear she's a son-of-a-gun."

Noah asked, "Gonna try her tonight?"

"What ya think, Pa?" Tom asked.

"Well, I don't know. Do us good to get a little rest, especially Granma. But other ways, I'd kind of like to get across her an' settled into a job. Only got about 40 dollars left. I'll feel better when we're all working, an' a little money coming in."

Noah said lazily, "Like to just stay here. Like to lay

---

1. **tarpaulin** piece of canvas

here forever. Never get hungry an' never get sad."

Tom looked at the ragged peaks across the river and the Needles downstream and said, "Never seen a place where folks can live without fighting hard scrabble and rocks. Get to thinking they ain't no such country."

Two other campers joined the Joad party in the stream. Pa asked politely, "Going west?"

"Nope. We come from there. Going back home to Texas. We can't make no living in California."

Pa asked, "Can you make a living in Texas?"

"Nope. But at least we can starve to death with people we know, without a bunch of fellas hating us."

Pa said, "What makes them hate you?"

"They hate you 'cause they're scared. There's lots of beautiful farm land, but it's all owned by a few rich folks. Most of it is laying fallow.[2] If they don't want to work her, she ain't gonna get worked."

"Good land, you say? An' they ain't working her?"

"That's why they're scared. They know a hungry fellow is gonna get food even if he got to take it. They know that fallow land's a sin an' somebody gonna take it. What the hell! You never been called 'Okie' yet?"

Tom said, "Okie? What's that?"

"Well, Okie used to mean you was from Oklahoma. Now it means you're a dirty son-of-a-she-dog. Okie means you're scum. Don't mean nothing itself, it's the way they say it. But I can't tell you nothing. You got to go there. I hear there's 300,000 of our people there— an' living like hogs, 'cause everything in California is owned. They ain't nothing left."

Pa looked at Uncle John and said, "What you think about this here?"

---

2. **fallow**   farming land that has been left unfarmed during the growing season.

Uncle John said, "We're going there, ain't we? None of this here talk gonna keep us from going."

Tom asked, "We going on tonight, Pa?"

"Might's well. Might's well get her over."

Tom walked in among the willows, and he crawled into some shade to lie down. Noah followed him.

"Gonna sleep here," Tom said.

Noah said, "Tom, I ain't going on."

Tom sat up. "What do you mean?"

"Tom, I ain't gonna leave this here water. I'm gonna walk on down this here river."

"You're crazy," Tom said.

"Get myself a piece of line. I'll catch fish. Fellow can't starve beside a nice river."

Tom said, "How about the family? How about Ma?"

"I can't help it. I can't leave this here water." Noah's wide-set eyes were half closed. "You know how it is, Tom. You know how the folks are nice to me. But they don't really care for me."

"You're crazy."

"No, I ain't. I know how I am. I know they're sorry. But—well, I ain't going. You tell Ma, Tom."

"Now, you look here," Tom began.

"No, it ain't no use. I was in that there water. An' I ain't gonna leave her. I'm gonna go now, Tom—down the river. I'll catch fish an' stuff, but I can't leave the river. I can't." He crawled back out of the willow cave. "You tell Ma, Tom." He walked away.

Tom followed him to the river bank. "Listen, you dang fool—"

"It ain't no use," Noah said. "I'm sad, but I can't help it. I got to go." He turned quickly and walked downstream along the shore. Tom started to follow, and then he stopped. He saw Noah disappear into the brush, and then appear again, following the edge of the river. And he watched Noah growing smaller on the edge of the river, until he disappeared into the willows at last. Tom took off his hat and scratched his head. He went back into his willow cave and lay down to sleep.

Tom slept until the sun sank low in the afternoon, then went to find his mother. "Ma, I got something to tell ya," he said. "Noah—he went on down the river. He ain't going on."

"Why?" she asked softly. Then Ma was silent a long time. "Family's falling apart," she said and turned her stunned eyes toward the river. "I don't know. Seems like I can't think no more. I just can't think. There's too much."

Tom said lamely, "He'll be all right, Ma. He's a funny kind of fellow." Then Pa came trooping up from the willows, his eyes still full of sleep.

"Ain't going?" Pa said. "What the hell's the matter with him?" Then he caught himself. "My fault," he said miserably. "That boy's all my fault." And he refused to talk about it any more.

Tom summoned Ruthie and Winfield and said, "You two go around an' tell everyone we're gonna get rolling soon as we can."

Wilson walked near for the last words and said, "We can't go, folks. Sairy's done up. She got to rest. She ain't gonna get across that desert alive." Jim Casy joined the group. Wilson turned to him and said, "Sairy wants you should go see her."

"Sure," said the preacher. He walked to the Wilson tent and went inside the dusky tent. Sairy lay on the mattress, her eyes wide and bright.

"I want you should say a prayer for me," she said.

He shook his head as though to awaken himself. "I don't understand this here," he said.

And she replied, "Yes—you know, don't you?"

"I know," he said, "I know, but I don't understand. Maybe you'll rest a few days an' then come on."

She shook her head slowly from side to side. "I'm just pain covered with skin. I know what it is, but I won't tell him. He'd be too sad. He wouldn't know what to do. Maybe in the night, when he's sleeping—when he waked up, it won't be so bad."

He offered to stay, but she said no, so he said a prayer. When he finished, he looked down at her, into her eyes, and said, "Good-bye."

The men loaded Granma, mattress and all, on the top of the truck. Granma still slept, her mouth wide open, and did not waken. The family climbed on the truck, Ma on top, beside Granma. Tom and Al and Pa in the seat, and Winfield on Pa's lap. Connie and Rose of Sharon made a nest against the cab. The preacher and Uncle John and Ruthie were in a tangle on top of the loaded truck.

Pa called, "Good-by, Mister and Mis' Wilson." There was no answer from the tent. Tom started the engine and the truck lumbered away.

The truck moved on into the evening, and the edge of the sun struck the rough horizon and turned the desert red. The dusk passed into dark and the desert stars came out in the soft sky. The lights of the truck came on, and they lit up a little blur of highway ahead and a strip of desert on either side of the road.

The truck moved on over the hot earth, and the hours passed. Ruthie and Winfield went to sleep. Ma lay on the mattress beside Granma. She could feel the struggling body and the struggling heart. The sobbing

breath was in her ear. And Ma said over and over, "All right. It's gonna be all right." And she said hoarsely, "You know the family got to get across."

Around midnight they stopped at an inspection station. An officer put down the license number and raised the hood.

Tom asked, "What's this here?"

"We got to look over your stuff," an officer said. "You got to unload."

"We got to get going," said Ma. "We got a sick ol' lady."

The officer shot a flashlight beam on Granma's old shrunken face.

"Go on ahead," he said.

They drove through Tehachapi in the morning glow, and the sun came up behind them. Then, suddenly, they saw the great valley below them. The vineyards, the orchards, the great flat valley, green and beautiful, the trees set in rows, and the farm houses. Al pulled to the side of the road and parked.

Pa said, "God Almighty! I never knowed they was anything like this." The peach trees and the walnut groves, and the dark green patches of oranges. And red roofs among the trees, and barns—rich barns. Al got out and stretched his legs.

He called, "Ma—come look. We're there!"

Ma got down. Her knees buckled and she sat on the running board. "Thank God!" she said. "The family's here." Al asked about Granma. Ma looked down at her hands, fingers entwined in her lap. "I wished I could wait an' not tell you. I wished it could be all—nice."

Pa said, "Then Granma's bad."

Ma raised her eyes and looked over the valley. "Granma's dead."

They all looked at her, and Pa asked, "When?"

"Middle of the night. I was afraid we wouldn't get across," Ma said. "I told Granma we couldn't help her. The family had to get across. I told her, told her when she was dying. We couldn't stop in the desert. There were the young ones—an' Rosasharn's baby. I told her." She covered her face with her hands for a moment. "She can get buried in a nice green place," Ma said softly. "Trees around an' a nice place. She got to lay her head down in California."

The family got back on the truck. Tom and Ma and Pa rode up front. The heavy truck moved, snorting and jerking and popping down the hill. The sun was behind them, and the valley golden and green before them. Ma shook her head slowly from side to side. "It's pretty," she said. "I wished they could of saw it."

"I wished so, too," said Pa. And the truck rolled down the mountain into the great valley.

Chapter 7

Once California belonged to Mexico; and its lands to Mexicans; and a horde of tattered feverish Americans poured in. And such was their hunger for land that they took the land—stole the land, those frantic hungry men; and they guarded with guns the land they had stolen.

Then, with time, the squatters were no longer squatters, but owners. Their children grew up and had children on the land. Farming became an industry. And all the time the farms grew larger and the owners fewer. And then the migrants flowed into California.

A man drove his old car into town, his wife beside him and his thin children in the back seat. He had scoured the farms for work. Where can we sleep tonight? Well, there's Hooverville[1] on the edge of the river. There's a whole raft of Okies there. He drove his old car to Hooverville. There was a Hooverville on the edge of every town.

The rag town lay close to the water; and the houses were tents, and weed-thatched shacks, paper houses, a great junk pile. The man drove his family in and became a citizen of Hooverville—always, the camps were called Hooverville.

When Pa and Ma and Uncle John came out of the coroner's office in Bakersfield, they were subdued and quiet. Uncle John climbed up on the back of the truck.

---

1. **Hooverville** town of temporary shacks used for housing during the Great Depression; named after President Herbert Hoover

Pa and Ma got into the front seat with Tom. Pa sighed deeply. "There wasn't nothing else to do," he said.

"I know," said Ma. "Granma would have liked a nice funeral, though. She always wanted one."

Pa turned to Ma. "You ain't to feel bad. We just didn't have it; embalming, an' a coffin, an' a preacher, an' a plot in a graveyard. It would a took ten times what we got. We done the best we could."

"I know," Ma said. "I just can't get it out of my head what store she set by a nice funeral. Got to forget it."

Tom started the car and they rolled through the streets and out toward the country. And by a bridge they saw a group of tents and shacks. Tom said, "Might as well stop here. Find out what's doing and where the work is." He drove down a steep dirt bank and parked next to the camp.

There was no order in the camp; little gray tents, shacks, cars were scattered about at random. In front of one of the tents stood an old Buick with the hood up. A young man was grinding the valves. The young man left his work and walked over to greet the Joads. "How are ya?" he said. "Welcome to Hooverville. You folks just come across?"

"We just got in," Tom said.

Pa said, "Can we just pull up anywheres an' camp?"

"Sure. Why not?" the young man said.

Ma said, "Let's get the camp up. I'm tired out. Maybe we can all rest." Pa and Uncle John climbed up on the truck to unload the canvas and the beds. Tom walked back to the Buick with the young man.

"We're looking for work," Tom said. We'll take any kind of work."

The young man looked at Tom in amazement. "Looking for work?" he said. "What you think everybody else is looking for? Diamonds?"

Tom looked about at the grimy tents, the junk equipment, at the old cars, the lumpy mattresses out in the sun, at the blackened cans on fire-blackened holes where the people cooked. He asked quietly, "Ain't there no work?"

"Ain't no crop right here now. Grapes an' cotton to pick later. We heard they was work up north. Soon's I get these here valves ground, me an' my wife an' my kids are heading north for Salinas."

Tom said, "Back home some fellas came through with some handbills—orange ones. Says they need lots of people out here to work the crops."

The young man laughed. "They say there's 300,000 of us folks here, an' I bet every damn family seen them handbills."

"If they don't need folks, what'd they go to the trouble of puttin' them things out for?"

"Look," the young man said. "Suppose you got a job an' there's just one fella wants the job. You got to pay him what he asks. But suppose there's 100 men wants that job—100 men dead broke with hungry kids to feed. Use your head, why don't you? You can print a lot of handbills with what you save paying 15 cents an hour for field work."

Tom said, "That's stinking."

The young man laughed harshly. "You stay out here a little while, an' if you smell any roses, you come an' let me smell, too."

Pa and Uncle John gathered wood for a fire and Ma got busy fixing a stew. Tom walked around to the other side of the tent and found the preacher there. Tom sat down beside him.

Casy sniffed the good stew smells and spoke softly to Tom. "I ain't doing nobody no good. Me or nobody else. I was thinking I'd go off alone by myself. I'm eating your food an' taking up room. An' I ain't giving you nothing. Maybe I could get a steady job an' maybe pay back some of the stuff you've given me."

Tom stared over the camp, over the gray tents and the shacks of weed and tin and paper. "Don't go away right yet," he said. "Not right yet."

"Quicker I get looking for work—quicker I'm gonna find some."

Tom studied him with half-shut eyes and said, "Something's going to happen here, I can sense it. So, stick around till tomorrow."

Casy watched him intently, started to ask a question, and then shut his mouth tightly. "Yeah, I won't go right yet," he said.

Tom settled back on his elbow and closed his eyes. Inside the tent he could hear the murmur of Rose of Sharon's voice and Connie's answering.

"I ought to help Ma," Rose of Sharon said, "but every time I stir I almost throw up."

"If I'd have known it would be like this I wouldn't have came," Connie said sullenly. "I'd a-studied nights about tractors back home an' got me a three-dollar job. Fellow can live awful nice on three dollars a day, an' go to a pitcher show every night, too."

Rose of Sharon looked scared. "You promised you're gonna study nights about radios," she said. He was long in answering. "Ain't you?" she demanded.

"Yeah, sure. Soon's I get on my feet."

She sat up. "You ain't givin' it up!"

"No—no—'course not. But—I didn't know they was places like this we got to live in."

The girl's eyes hardened. "You got to," she said. "We got to have a house before the baby comes. We ain't gonna have this baby in no field."

"Sure," he said. "Soon as I get on my feet."

The sun was sinking now, and the yellow sunlight fell on Hooverville and on the willows behind it. A new Chevrolet turned off the highway and headed down into camp. It pulled to the center of the camp. A man wearing khaki pants, a flannel shirt, and a Stetson hat got out of the car. His companion stayed seated.

The man said, "You men want to work?" The migrant men looked at him quietly, suspiciously. And men from all over camp moved near.

One of the migrant men spoke at last. "Sure we wanta work. Where's the work?"

"Tulare County. Fruit's opening up. Need pickers."

A young migrant named Floyd Knowles spoke up. "You doing the hiring?"

A man in overalls asked, "What you paying?"

"About 30 cents. Can't tell exactly yet."

"You got the work. Why can't you tell?"

The khaki man said, "The pay's keyed to the price of the fruit. Might be a little more, might be a little less."

Floyd stepped out ahead. He said quietly, "I'll go, mister. You're a contractor, an' you got a license. You just show your license, an' then you give us an order to go to work, an' where, an' when, an' how much we'll get, an' you sign that, an' we'll all go."

The contractor turned, scowling. "You telling me how to run my own business?"

Floyd said, "If we're working for you, it's our business too."

"Well, you ain't telling me what to do. I told you I need men."

Floyd said angrily, "You didn't say how many men, an' you didn't say what you'd pay."

"Dang it, I don't know yet."

"If you don't know, you got no right to hire men."

"I got a right to run my own business my own way. I'm out getting men for Tulare County. Going to need a lot of men."

Floyd spoke to the crowd. "Twice now I've fell for that. Maybe he needs 1,000 men. He'll get 5,000 there, an' he'll pay 15 cents an hour. An' you poor slobs'll have to take it 'cause you'll be hungry. If he wants to hire men, let him hire them an' write out an' say what he's gonna pay. Ask to see his license. He ain't allowed to contract men without a license."

The contractor turned to the Chevrolet and called, "Joe!" His companion stepped out. He wore riding breeches and laced boots. A heavy pistol holster hung on a cartridge belt around his waist. A deputy sheriff's star was pinned to his brown shirt. His face was set to a thin smile.

"What do you want?" he asked.

The contractor pointed to Floyd and said, "Ever see this guy before, Joe?"

"Hmm, seems like I seen this fellow hanging around last week when that used-car lot got busted into." The smile left his face, and he unhooked the strap that covered the butt of his automatic. "Get in that car," he said to Floyd.

Tom said, "You got nothing on him."

The deputy swung around. "If you'd like to go in too, you just open your trap once more. They was two fellows hanging around that lot."

"I wasn't even in the state last week," Tom said.

"Well, maybe you're wanted someplace else. You keep your trap shut."

The contractor turned back to the men. "You fellas don't want to listen to these darn reds.[2]

---

2. **red** member of the Communist Party, especially a labor activist

Troublemakers—they'll get you in trouble. Now I can use all of you in Tulare County."

The men didn't answer.

The deputy turned back to them. "Might be a good idea to go to Tulare," he said. The thin smile was back on his face. "Board of Health says we got to clean out this camp. An' if it gets around that you got reds out here—why, somebody might get hurt. That's just a friendly way of telling you to clear out of here. Be a bunch a guys down here, maybe with pick handles, if you ain't gone."

The contractor said, "I told you I need men. If you don't want to work—well, that's your business."

The deputy smiled. "If you don't want to work, there ain't a place for you in this county. I don't want one of you here by tomorrow morning."

The contractor stepped into the Chevrolet.

"Now, you," the deputy said to Floyd, "you get in that car." He took hold of Floyd's arm. Floyd spun and swung with one movement. His fist splashed into the large face, and in the same motion he was away, dodging down the line of tents. The deputy staggered and Tom put out his foot for him to trip over. The deputy fell heavily and rolled, reaching for his gun.

Floyd dodged in and out of sight down the line. The deputy fired from the ground. Far down the line Floyd came in sight, sprinting for the willows. The deputy, sitting on the ground, raised his gun again and then, suddenly, from the group of men, the Reverend Casy stepped. He kicked the deputy in the neck and stood back as the heavy man crumpled into unconsciousness.

The motor of the Chevrolet roared and it streaked away, churning dust to the highway and shooting off.

Casy moved close to Tom. "You got to get out," he said. "You go down in the willows an' wait. He didn't see me kick him, but he saw you stick out your foot."

"I don't want to go," Tom said.

Casy drew close and whispered, "They'll fingerprint you. You broke parole. They'll send you back."

Tom drew in his breath quietly. "Geez! I forgot."

"Go quick," Casy said. "If it's all right to come back, I'll give you four high whistles."

Tom strolled away casually, but as soon as he was away from the group he hurried his steps, and he disappeared among the willows that lined the river.

Al stepped over the fallen deputy. "Geez," he said admiringly, "you sure flagged him down."

Casy turned to Al. "Get out," he said. "Go on, get out—to the tent. You don't know nothing."

"Yeah? How about you?"

Casy grinned at him. "Somebody got to take the blame. I got no kids. They'll just put me in jail, an' I ain't doing nothing but set around."

Four armed deputies arrived soon and hauled Casy away. He walked off proudly, his head up. On his lips was a faint smile and on his face a curious look of triumph.

When the sound of sirens faded in the distance, Rose of Sharon moved dizzily out of the Joads' tent. "Where's Connie?" she asked irritably. "I ain't seen Connie for a long time. Where'd he go?"

"I ain't seen him," said Ma. "If I see him, I'll tell him you want him."

Ma looked at the girl's swollen face. "You been crying," she said.

The tears started freshly in Rose of Sharon's eyes.

Ma went on firmly. "You get a hold of yourself. There's a lot of us here. Come here now an' peel some potatoes. You're feeling sorry for yourself."

The girl started to go back in the tent. She tried to

avoid Ma's stern eyes, but they made her turn slowly toward the fire. "He shouldn't have went away," she said, but the tears were gone. And her eyes blazed with resentment.

"You seen Connie?" she asked Al.

"Yeah," said Al. "Way to hell an' gone up the river. He's going south."

"Was—was he going away?"

Ma turned to the girl. "Rosasharn, you been talking an' acting funny. What'd Connie say to you?"

"Said it would a been a good thing if he stayed home an' studied up tractors," Rose of Sharon said.

Pa said, "Connie wasn't no good. All the time saying what he's gonna do. Never doing nothing. I didn't want to say nothing while he's here. But now he's run out—"

"Sh!" Ma said softly.

"Why for God's sake? Why do I got to shh? He run out, didn't he?"

Ma said, "Rosasharn gonna have a little fella an' that baby is half Connie. It ain't good for a baby to grow up with folks saying his pa ain't no good."

"Better than lying about it," said Pa.

Rose of Sharon got up and went into the tent.

"We got no time for talking," Tom broke in. "We got to be on our way."

"We just come here," said Ma.

"They're going to burn the camp tonight," said Tom.

Ma made her decision. "Come on!" she said. "We got to be quick."

Pa said, "How about John?"

"Where is Uncle John?" Tom asked.

"He went to get drunk," Pa said.

"Where'd he go?" Tom asked.

"I don't know," said Pa. Tom found Uncle John down the bank. He lifted the sagging body and carried it home. The truck was loaded and ready.

Tom asked, "Where's Rosasharn?" Ma pointed toward her.

Tom walked over and said, "Come on. We got to go."

"I want Connie. I ain't going till he gets back."

Tom said, "Connie'll find us. I left word up at the store where we'd be."

"I want to wait."

"We can't wait." Ma leaned down and took the girl by the arm and helped her to her feet.

"Maybe he went to get them books to study up on," said the girl. "Maybe he was gonna surprise us."

Ma said, "Maybe that's just what he done." They led Rose of Sharon to the truck and helped her on board.

Tom drove out to Highway 99 and turned south. Ma asked, "Where we going, Tom?"

"Gonna look for a government camp over by Weedpatch," Tom said. "Fellow said they don't let no deputies in there. Ma—I got to get away from them. I'm scared I'll kill one."

The dim lights moved along the broad black highway.

Chapter

The truck jiggled along slowly. Tom drove in silence. Ma said, "Girl back at the Hooverville told me about the government camp."

"What'd she say?" Tom asked.

"Said it's got nice toilets an' baths, an you can wash clothes in a tub, an' there's water right handy, good drinking water; an' nights the folks play music an' Saturday night they give a dance."

"Sounds nice."

"An' she said it's got a place for kids to play, an' them toilets with paper," Ma went on. "Pull down a little jigger an' the water comes right in the toilet, an' they ain't no cops let to come look in your tent any time they want. An' folks is nice there."

It was late when Tom Joad drove along a country road several miles south of Bakersfield and found the Weedpatch camp. A high wire fence faced the road, and a wire-gated driveway turned in. A little way inside the gate there was a small house with a light in the window. Tom turned in. A watchman stood up from the porch and walked to the car.

Tom asked, "You got any room here for us?"

"Got one camp. How many of you?"

Tom counted on his fingers. "Me, an' Pa, an' Ma, Al an' Rosasharn, an' Uncle John, an' Ruthie an' Winfield. Them last is kids."

The watchman directed Tom to a camp site and said, "You'll be in Number Four Sanitary Unit."

"What's that?"

"Toilets and showers and wash tubs."

Ma demanded, "You got wash tubs—running water?"

"Sure."

"Oh! Praise God," said Ma.

"The camp costs a dollar a week," the watchman said, "but you can work it out, carrying garbage, keeping the camp clean—stuff like that."

"We'll work it out," said Tom.

"You'll see the committee tomorrow. They'll show you how to use the camp and tell you the rules."

"Committee?"

"There's five sanitary units," said the watchman. "Each one elects a Central Committee man. Now, that committee makes the laws. What they say goes."

"Suppose they get tough," Tom said.

"Well, you can vote them out just as quick as you can vote 'em in, but they do a fine job, an' it works."

"Ma's gonna like this place," Tom said. "She ain't been treated decent for a long time."

A small clang brought Tom from sleep. He stood up and looked down the row of tents. Grey smoke spurted from a fire. He moved closer. A girl was frying bacon. "Morning," she said.

Two men came out of the tent. "Had your breakfast?" the older one asked Tom.

"Well, no, I ain't."

"Well, sit down with us. We got plenty. Been working for 12 days. Working, getting our pay, and eating."

"Look," said the younger man, "we're laying pipe. Maybe we could get you on."

"Just wait a minute," Tom said. "I'll tell my folks."

Ruthie was the only one up. "You tell them I got a chance at a job," Tom said. Ruthie nodded.

Tom and the men walked down a graveled road to a

small orchard. "Morning, Mr. Thomas," the younger man said. "This here's Tom Joad. Can you put him on?"

"Oh, sure. I'll put him on. I'll put everybody on."

"We just thought—"

"I been thinking too. I been paying you 30 cents an hour, that right?"

"Why, sure, but—"

"And getting 30 cents of work. But now I'm paying you 25 cents. You ever hear of the Farmers' Association? Well, we had a meeting last night. You know who owns the Association? The Bank of the West. So last night the member from the bank says I'd better cut it down to 25. I said, 'The men are worth 30.' And he says, 'The wage is 25 now. By the way, you going to need a crop loan next year?' You see? The rate is 25 cents—and like it."

Mr. Thomas looked at the men. "You live in that government camp, right? I'm gonna tell you something. The Association don't like the government camps. Can't get a deputy in there. The people make their own laws, I hear, and you can't arrest a man without a warrant. Now if there were a big fight and maybe a shooting—a bunch of deputies could go in and clean out the camp.

"Forget where you heard it, but there's going to be a fight in the camp Saturday night. And there's going to be deputies ready to go in."

Tom demanded. "Why, for God's sake? Those folks ain't bothering nobody."

"I'll tell you why," Mr. Thomas said. "Those folks in the camp are getting used to being treated like human beings. When they go back to the squatters' camps, they'll be hard to handle." He paused, then said, "Geez, I hope I haven't talked myself out of my farm. But I like you people."

The sun came over the mountains, and the camp woke up. Ma went to the showers and looked in. She ran her finger over the white porcelain of the wash basins. Then she washed her hands in the warm water, and she washed her face.

When Saturday afternoon came, the whole camp quickened and the people grew excited. In the tent of Ezra Huston, chairman, the Central Committee of five men went into a meeting. Huston, a tall spare man, wind-blackened, with eyes like little blades, spoke to his committee. "It's damn lucky we got the word they was gonna try to bust up the dance," he said.

Now the tubby little representative from Unit Three spoke up. "I think we oughta squash heck out of them, an' show them."

"No," said Huston. "That's what they want. No, sir. If they can get a fight going, then they can run in the cops an' say we ain't orderly. They tried it before— other places." He turned to the sad, dark boy from Unit Two. "Got the fellows together to go round the fences an' see nobody sneaks in?"

The sad boy nodded. "Yeah. Twelve. Told them not to hit nobody. Just push them out again."

Huston said, "How about you, Willie Eaton? You're chairman of the entertainment, ain't you?"

Willie Eaton grinned happily. "Well, sir, ordinary entertainment committee is five. I got 20 more—all good strong boys. They're gonna be dancing an' keeping their eyes open an' their ears open. First sign— any talk or argument, they close in tight. Worked her out pretty nice. Can't even see nothing. Kind of move out, an' the fellow will go out with them."

Willie Eaton came to the tent. "You Tom Joad?"

"Yeah."

"We need you. Want you to look over the guys when they come in," he said, "an' try to spot any trouble-makers. Then later I want you to dance an' watch."

"Yeah! I can do that all right," said Tom.

Before the dance started, Tom told Ma, "I'm on a committee. We're gonna entertain some fellows."

"Already on a committee?" Ma said. "I guess it's 'cause you got work."

Rose of Sharon, helping Ma with the supper dishes, turned to put one away. Tom pointed at her. "My God, she's getting big," he said.

Rose of Sharon blushed. "Sure she is," Ma said.

"An' she's getting prettier," said Tom.

"Girl with a baby always gets prettier," said Ma.

Tom laughed. "If she keeps swelling like this, she gonna need a wheelbarrow to carry it."

"Now you stop," Rose of Sharon said, and she went inside the tent, out of sight.

Ma chuckled, "You shouldn't ought to worry her."

"She likes it," said Tom.

"I know she likes it, but it worries her, too. And she's mourning for Connie."

"Well, she might as well give him up. He's probably studying to be President of the United States by now."

"Don't worry her," Ma said. "She ain't got no easy row to hoe."

When Tom left, Ma went to Rose of Sharon and said, "Tom was only jollying you."

"I know. I didn't mind; only I hate to have folks look at me." Then she sighed and said desperately, "I don' know what I'm gonna do, Ma. I just don't know."

Ma put her two hands on Rose of Sharon's hair. "You're a good girl," she said. "You always was a good girl. I'll take care of you. Don't you fret."

When the fiddlers struck up the music for the second square dance, Tom saw three strangers force their way through, toward some of the dancers. Twenty young men lounged slowly across the floor. Off in the darkness, a shrill whistle sounded. The three were walled in now. And each one felt the grip of hands. And then the wall of men moved slowly off the dance platform.

A touring car drove to the entrance. The driver called, "Open up. We hear you got a riot."

"We got no riot here."

The men listened to the music and then the car pulled slowly away and waited.

"Listen you," said Willie Eaton to the three strangers. "We're letting you off this time. But you take back the word. If this ever happens again, we'll bust every bone in their body."

They neared the fence. "Got some fellows going home early," said Willie. The three men climbed over the fence and disappeared into the darkness. The music of "Old Dan Tucker" whined from the string band.

Chapter 9

The spring is beautiful in California. The full green hills are round and soft as water-filled balloons. And on the level lands are the mile-long rows of pale green lettuce and the spindly little cauliflowers, the gray-green artichoke plants.

And then the leaves break out on the trees, and the petals drop from the fruit trees and carpet the earth with pink and white. The centers of the blossoms swell and grow and color: cherries and apples, peaches and pears. All California quickens with produce, and the limbs bend gradually under the fruit.

First the cherries ripen. Cent and a half a pound. Hell, we can't pick them for that. The purple prunes soften and sweeten. My God, we can't pick them. We can't pay wages, no matter what wages.

The little farmers watched debt creep up on them like the tide. This little orchard will be part of a great holding next year, for the debt will have choked the owner. This little vineyard will belong to the bank. Only the great owners will survive, for they own the canneries, too. And four pears peeled and cut in half, cooked and canned, still cost 15 cents. And canned pears do not spoil. They will last for years.

The decay spreads over the state, and the sweet smell is a great sorrow on the land. The fruits of the trees will be destroyed to keep up the price. Carloads of oranges dumped on the ground. And men with hoses squirt kerosene on the oranges. A million people hungry, needing the fruit—and kerosene sprayed over the golden mountains.

The migrant workers and their families are slowly

starving. And, in the eyes of the hungry, there is a growing wrath.[1] In the souls of the people, the grapes of wrath are filling and growing heavy, growing heavy for the vintage.[2]

In the Weedpatch camp, the Joad family lingered after their supper. Ma hesitated before she started to do the dishes.

"We got to do something," she said. And she pointed at Winfield. "Look at him," she said. And when they stared at the little boy, "He's jerking an' twisting in his sleep. Look at his color." The members of the family looked at the earth in shame. "Fried dough," Ma said. "One month we been here. An' Tom had five days' work. An' the rest of you scrabbling out every day, an' no work. An' scared to talk. An' the money gone. You're scared to talk it out. Every night you just eat, then you get wandering away. Can't bear to talk it out. Well, you got to. Rosasharn ain't far from due, an' look at her color. You got to talk it out. Now don't none of you get up till we figure something out. One day's more grease an' two days' flour, an' ten potatoes. You set here an' get busy."

Pa said, "We been looking, Ma. Been going in every gate, walking up to every house, even when we knew they wasn't gonna be nothing. Puts a weight on you. Going out looking for something you know you ain't gonna find."

Ma said fiercely, "You ain't got the right to get discouraged. This here family's going under. You just ain't got the right."

Uncle John said, "Fellow says there's cotton coming

1. **wrath** anger
2. **vintage** crop of grapes

in up north, near a place called Tulare. That ain't very far, the fellow says."

"Well, we got to get going, an' going quick. I ain't setting here no longer, no matter how nice." Ma took up her bucket and left to fetch hot water.

"Ma gets tough," Tom said. "I see her getting mad now. She just boils up."

Pa said with relief, "Well, she brought it into the open, anyways. Now we can talk her out."

Ma came back with her bucket of steaming water. "Well," she demanded, "figger anything out?"

Tom said, "You win. We'll move on in the morning."

North of Bakersfield, there came a harsh hissing noise from the front of the truck. The truck bumped to a stop. "If there's one nail in the county, we run over it," Tom said.

Tom and Al worked well together. Tom was pumping at the tire when a car coming from the north stopped on the other side of the road. A brown-faced man dressed in a light gray business suit got out and walked across to the truck.

"Morning," he said pleasantly. "You people looking for work?"

"We sure are, mister," said Tom.

"Can you pick peaches?" the man asked.

"We can pick anything there is."

"Well, you go north to Pixley, that's 35 or 36 miles, and you turn east. Ask anybody where the Hooper ranch is. You'll find plenty of work there."

Ma said excitedly, "With four men working maybe I can get some credit right off. First thing I'll get is coffee, cause you been wanting that, and then some flour and baking powder and some meat. And soap. Got to get soap. Wonder where we'll stay." She babbled on.

"And milk. I'll get some milk 'cause Rosasharn, she ought to have milk."

The sun moved up toward noon and the shadow of the truck grew lean and moved under the wheels. "Must be Pixley up the road," Al said. They drove into town and turned eastward on a narrower road. And the orchards lined the way and made an aisle.

Far ahead the road was blocked with cars, and a line of white motorcycles was drawn up along the roadside. As they drew near, a state policeman stepped around the last parked car and held up his hand. Al pulled to a stop. The policeman leaned on the side of the car. "Where you going?"

Al said, "Fellow said they was work picking peaches up this way."

"Want to work, do you?"

"Damn right," said Tom.

"OK. Wait a minute." He moved to the side of the road and called ahead. "One more. That's six cars ready. Better take this batch through."

Tom called, "Hey! What's the matter?"

"Got a little trouble up ahead, but you'll get through," the officer said. "Just follow the line."

The line of cars moved on, with the Joad truck last. Two motorcycles led the way, two followed. The column roared past a line of men standing in a ditch beside the road. Tom saw their mouths open as though they were yelling, saw their shaking fists and their furious faces. "These here is our own people, all of them," Tom said. "I don't like this."

Suddenly the leading policeman turned off the road into a wide graveled entrance. The old cars whipped after them. A high wire gate swung open. The six old cars moved through and the gate closed behind them. The four motorcycles turned and sped back toward town. Now the distant yelling of the men in the ditch could be heard. Two men stood beside the graveled road. Each one carried a shotgun.

The six cars moved ahead to the peach camp. There were 50 little square, flat-roofed boxes, each with a door and a window, and the whole group in a square. At the end of each row of square houses stood two men armed with shotguns and wearing big silver stars pinned to their shirts.

The six cars stopped. Two bookkeepers moved from car to car. "How many want to work?"

Tom answered, "Eight, but what is this?"

"That's not your affair. Find house 63. Wages 5 cents a box. No bruised fruit. All right, move along now. Get to work right away."

The Joads unloaded their belongings in house 63. The floor was splashed with grease. In the one room stood a rusty stove and nothing more. The room smelled of sweat and grease. Rose of Sharon stood beside Ma. "We gonna live here?"

Ma was silent for a moment. "Why sure," she said at last. "It ain't so bad once we wash an' mop it out."

The menfolk went on down to the orchard and began filling their buckets with globes of gold and red from the tree branches, while the women stayed behind to clean house 63. The men worked on through the afternoon. Ruthie and Winfield joined them after a while and Pa put them to work, too. In mid-afternoon Ma came trudging out. "I would have come before, but Rosasharn fainted," she said. "Just fainted away."

When the sun went down they had picked 20 boxes. Tom set the twentieth box down. "A buck," he said. "How long do we work?"

"Work till dark, long as you can see," Pa said.

Ma left early to get fixings for supper at the company store, where they could buy on credit. Tom and Al and Pa and Uncle John walked in from the orchard when the dusk was deep. Their feet were heavy against the road.

"You wouldn't think just reaching up an' picking would get you in the back," Pa said.

"Be all right in a couple of days," said Tom. "Say, Pa, after we eat I'm gonna walk out an' see what all that fuss is outside the gate. Want to come?"

"No," said Pa, "I'm just gonna set awhile, an' then go to bed."

The fire roared in the Joad house. Hamburger patties splashed and hissed in the grease, and the potatoes bubbled. They ate silently, wolfishly, and wiped up the grease with their bread. And they were still hungry when they finished. But there was no more food.

Ma said, "That's all. You made a dollar, an' that's a dollars worth. Tomorrow, you'll get in a full day. Tomorrow night, we'll have plenty."

After supper, Tom strolled off down the street. When he reached the State Road, an armed guard with a flashlight stopped him and ordered him to turn back. "It's for your own good," he said. "Them crazy pickets might get you."

"What pickets?"

"Them damn reds. You better get along back."

"That's OK with me, mister." Tom swung about and started back. He walked in a different direction, off into the stubble field beside the highway. A stream cut across the fields, and the highway crossed it on a small concrete bridge. Tom looked over the side of the bridge. At the bottom of the bank he saw a tent. A lantern was burning. He moved down through the brush and approached the tent. A man sat on a box in front of the tent.

"Evening," Tom said.

"Who are you?"

"Well—I guess, well—I'm just going past."

"Know anybody here?"

"No, I tell you I was just going past."

A head stuck out of the tent. A voice said, "What's the matter?"

"Casy!" Tom cried. "Casy! For crying out loud, what you doing here?"

"Why, my God, it's Tom Joad! Come on in, Tommy."

"Know him, do you?" the man in front asked.

"Know him? Hell, yes. Known him for years. I came west with him. Come on in, Tom."

Casy introduced Tom to three other men in the tent. A dark-faced scowling man held out his hand. "I heard what Casy said. This the fellow you was telling about?"

"Sure. This is him. Well, for God's sake! Where's your folks? What you doing here?"

"We heard there was work here," Tom said. "But when we come in I seen a bunch of fellows yelling. They wouldn't tell me nothing, so I come out here to see what's going on. How'd you get here?"

The preacher leaned forward and said, "Jail house is a funny place. Here's me, been traveling in the wilderness like Jesus to try to find out something. But it's in the jail that I found my calling, my real calling. I talked to everyone in that big jail."

"'Course you did," said Tom. "If you was up on the gallows you'd be passing the time of day with the hangman. Never seen such a talker."

The men in the tent chuckled.

Casy grinned and went on. "Well, sir, I begin getting at things. Most of them fellows in jail got there for stealing things they needed an' couldn't get no other way. Them rich owners been cheating them so bad they didn't have no choice except to starve. All a sudden, I knew my true calling was to help them poor folks fight back."

The outside man stuck his head inside. "Casy, turn out that lantern an' come outside. There's something going on."

Casy said softly, "All of them is itchy. Them cops been saying how they're gonna beat the hell out of us and run us out of the county. They figger I'm a leader 'cause I talk so much."

"You ain't told me what's going on," Tom said.

"This here's a strike."[3]

"Why they striking? Five cents ain't much, but a fellow can eat," Tom said.

Casy said, "Look, Tom. We come to work here. They say it's gonna be five cents. Then it's two and a half. So we says we won't take it. When they bust this here strike, you think they'll pay five?"

"I don't know," Tom said.

"You got to tell them, Tom," Casy said.

"We was out of food. Think Pa's going to give up his meat for other fellows? And Rosasharn ought to get milk."

The man outside pulled the tent flap wide.

"Hear that?" the outside man said.

"I hear it," said Tom. There were sounds of faint footsteps from the road, a crunch of clods up on a bank, a little swish of brush down the stream. "I think they's guys coming from every which way. We better get out of here."

"Let's go," said Casy.

A sharp call. "There they are!" Two flashlight

---

3. strike when people stop work in order to protest unfair wages or working conditions.

beams fell on the men, caught them, blinded them. "Stand where you are." The voices came out of the dark. "That's him."

Casy stared blindly at the light. He breathed heavily. "Listen," he said. "You fellows don't know what you're doing. You're helping to starve kids."

"Shut up, you red son-of-a-bitch."

A short heavy man stepped into the light. He carried a new white pick handle.

Casy went on, "You don't know what you're doing."

The heavy man swung with the pick handle. Casy dodged down into the swing. The heavy club crashed into the side of his head with a dull crunch of bone. Casy fell sideways out of the light.

"Geez, George. I think you killed him."

"Put the light on him," said George. "Serve the son-of-a-bitch right." The flashlight beam dropped down and found Casy's crushed head.

Tom looked down at the preacher. The light crossed the heavy man's legs and the new white pick handle. Tom leaped silently. He wrenched the club free. The first time he knew he had missed and struck a shoulder, but the second time his crushing blow found the head. As the heavy man sank down, three more blows found his head. The lights danced about. There were shouts, the sound of running feet, crashing through the brush. Tom stood over the fallen man. And then a club reached his head, a glancing blow. He felt the stroke like an electric shock. And then he was running along the stream, bending low. Running.

A rooster crowed, far away, and gradually the window in house 63 lightened. Tom touched his swollen face with his fingertips. His nose was crushed and the blood was dried black on his lips and chin. The edges of the torn cheek were gathered and tight.

"Tom," Ma whispered, "what's the matter?"

Al woke up and said, "Geez! What was you in?"

"What's the matter?" Uncle John asked.

Tom braced himself on one elbow for a moment, and then he lay back. "Geez, I'm weak. I'm gonna tell you once. So I'll tell all of you." Ma started to send Ruthie and Winfield outside. "No," Tom said. "They got to hear. They might blab if they don't know."

"What the hell is this," Pa demanded.

"Last night I went out to see what all the yelling was about," Tom continued. "An' I come on Casy."

"The preacher?"

"Yeah, Pa. The preacher, only he was leading the strike. They come for him." Tom recounted the night's events. "They killed him. Busted his head. I was standing there an' I went nuts. Grabbed the pick handle." He paused, then said, "I—I clubbed the guy."

Ma's breath caught in her throat. Pa stiffened. "Kill him?" he asked softly.

"I—don't know. I was nuts. Tried to."

From the street came the sound of cars moving slowly. Pa stepped to the window and looked out. "There's a whole slew of new people coming in."

"Guess they busted the strike last night," said Tom. "Guess you'll start at only two an' a half cents now."

"Can't make enough to eat at that wage," said Pa.

"Well, what we gonna do?" Uncle John asked.

"We're gonna get while the gettin's good," said Ma, "before they come looking for Tom."

Pa and Al and Uncle John went into the orchard and worked all day. They told the fruit checker that Tom had taken sick. Ma and Rose of Sharon and Ruthie and Winfield loaded the truck during the day.

With Tom hidden under the mattresses, the Joad family headed out of Hooper ranch that evening.

A guard stopped them. "What's going on?"

"We're going out," said Pa. "Got a better job offer down by Weedpatch."

The guard shined his flashlight around the truck. "Wasn't there another fellow with you?"

Al said, "You mean that hitchhiker? Little short fella with a pale face?"

"Yeah. I guess that's what he looked like."

"He went away this morning when the rate dropped."

"OK," said the guard. And he swung the gate open.

Chapter 10

Cotton Pickers Wanted—signs on the road, handbills out, orange-colored handbills—Cotton Pickers Wanted.

The cars move to the cotton fields. The cotton camps set up. The screened high trucks and trailers are piled high with white fluff. Cotton clings to the fence wires, and cotton rolls in little balls along the road when the wind blows. And clean white cotton, going to the gin. And cotton clinging to your clothes and stuck to your whiskers. Blow your nose, there's cotton in your nose. Now into the cotton camp. Sidemeat tonight, by God!

Al turned right on a graveled road, and the yellow lights shuddered over the ground. The fruit trees were gone now, and cotton plants took their places. The road paralleled a bushy creek. Alongside the creek stood a long line of red boxcars, wheelless. A big sign beside the road said, "Cotton Pickers Wanted."

Al stopped. Tom said, "Maybe we can get work there an' live in one of them cars."

"How about you?" Ma demanded.

"I could hide in that brush an' keep out of sight," Tom said. "Soon as my face gets a little better, why, I'll come out an' go to picking."

"Well, all right," Ma agreed. "But don't you take no chances. Don't let nobody see you for a while."

Twelve boxcars stood end to end on a little flat beside the stream. They made good houses, with room for 24 families, one family in each end of each car. The Joads had one end of an end car. Someone had left an oil-can stove for cooking. Ma hung the canvas across the middle of the car, separating the Joads from the Wainwrights on the other side.

"It's nice," Ma said. "Almost nicer than anything we had except the government camp."

Each night they unrolled the mattresses on the floor, and each morning rolled them up again. And every day they went into the fields and picked cotton, 80 cents for 100 pounds, and every night they had meat. And every day Ma would sneak something out to Tom in his brush hideaway.

On Saturday they drove into Tulare, and they bought new overalls for the menfolk and a dress for Ma. And Ma splurged a dime on two large boxes of Cracker Jacks for Ruthie and Winfield.

Later, back at the boxcar camp, Winfield came breathless, running to Ma. "Ma—Ruthie told."

"Told what?"

"About Tom."

Ma stared. "Told?" Then she knelt in front of him. "Who'd she tell?"

"Some kids tried to get some of her Cracker Jacks, and Ruthie wouldn't give them none. So they got mad, and one kid grabbed her box. Then Ruthie got mad. She chased one, and one big girl hit her. Then Ruthie said she'd get her big brother. The girl said she'd get her big brother, too. An Ruthie said, 'Oh yeah? My brother's hiding right now from killing a fellow, and he can kill that big girl's brother, too.'"

"Oh, my," Ma said wearily. "What we gonna do now?" She put her forehead in her hand and rubbed her eyes.

That night, Ma stepped in among the willows beside the stream and found Tom. She handed him a tin plate wrapped in newspaper. "Pork chops an' fry potatoes."

"God Almighty, an' still warm," said Tom.

Ma said uneasily, "Tom—Ruthie told about you." She heard him gulp.

"Ruthie? What for?"

"Well, it wasn't her fault. You got to go away, Tom."

"Yeah. I knowed it from the start."

"We been makin' pretty good," she said. "I been putting money away. Here, take this seven dollars."

"I ain't gonna take your money. I'll get by."

Ma said, "I ain't gonna sleep none if you ain't got no money. Maybe you got to take a bus. Go to a big city like Los Angeles or San Francisco. They wouldn't never look for you there."

"Hm-m," he said. "Lookie, Ma, I been all day an' all night thinking 'bout what Casy said. Says he didn't have no soul that was his. Says his little piece of soul wasn't no good unless it was with the rest of the people, an' was whole. Funny how I remember."

"He was a good man," Ma said.

Tom said, "I been thinking, long as I'm an outlaw anyways, maybe I could—Hell, I ain't thought it out clear, but maybe I could help people like us somehow."

They sat silent in the coal-black cave of willows. "How am I gonna know about you?" Ma asked. "They might kill you an' I wouldn't know. How am I gonna know?"

Tom laughed uneasily. "Well, maybe like Casy says, a fella ain't got a soul of his own, but only a piece of a big one—an' then—"

"Then what, Tom?"

"Then it don't matter. I'll be around in the dark. I'll be everywhere—wherever you look. Wherever they's a fight so hungry people can eat, I'll be there. Wherever they's a cop beating up a guy, I'll be there. If Casy knowed, why, I'll be in the way guys yell when they're

mad an'—I'll be in the way kids laugh when they're hungry an' they know supper's ready. An' when our folks eat the stuff they raise an' live in the houses they build—why, I'll be there. See? God, I'm talkin' like Casy. Comes of thinkin' of him so much. Seems like I can see him sometimes."

"I don't understand," Ma said.

"Me neither," said Tom. "It's just stuff I been thinking about. You got to get back, Ma."

"You take the money, then."

He was silent for a moment. "All right," he said.

"An', Tom, later—when it's blowed over, you'll come back. You'll find us?"

"Sure," he said. "Now you better go." He squeezed her hand and said, "Good-by."

"Good-by," she said, and she walked quickly away. Her eyes were wet and burning, but she did not cry as she went back to the boxcar camp and the others.

Pa looked up when she entered and said, "Mr. Wainwright—he's got a worry he come to talk to us about."

"Our Aggie an' your boy Al's out walking every night," Wainwright said. "Suppose she got in trouble?"

Ma said softly, "We'll try an' see that we don't put no shame on you."

"Good night then, an' we sure thank you." He went around the curtain.

There were creeping steps behind the boxcar. Then Al came in. "Hello," he said. "I thought you'd be sleeping by now."

"Al," Ma said, "We're talking. Come sit down."

"I want to talk too. Me and Aggie Wainwright want to get married. We'll have to rent a house for a while. And—" he looked up fiercely, "nobody's gonna stop us!"

"Al," Ma said at last, "We're awful glad."

The rain began with gusty showers, pauses and downpours. Then it settled to a single tempo, small drops and a steady beat. In the boxcars, the families huddled together, listening to the pouring water on the roofs. And they were silent.

No work till spring. No work.

And if no work—no money, no food.

The women watched the men, watched to see if the break would come at last. The women stood silently and watched. And where a number of men gathered together, the fear went from their faces, and anger took its place. And the women sighed with relief, for they knew it was all right—the break had not come. It would never come, as long as fear could turn to wrath.

Tiny points of grass came through the earth, and in a few days the hills were pale green with the new year.

In the boxcar camp, the water stood in puddles, and the rain splashed in the mud. Gradually, the little stream crept up the bank toward the low flat where the boxcar stood. Pa squatted in the doorway of the boxcar the Joads and the Wainwrights shared. He watched the water rise. "Coming up fast," he said.

Wainwright said, "We was just talking. Seems like we ought to be getting out of here."

Al said, "Pa, if they go, I'm going too."

Pa looked startled. "You can't, Al. The truck—We ain't fit to drive that truck."

"I don't care. Me and Aggie got to stick together."

"Now, wait a minute." Pa pointed. "See? We just build a bank."

"Lot of work, an' then she might come over anyways," Wainwright said.

"We ain't gonna find us no nicer place to live than this. We can do it if everybody helps."

Al said, "If Aggie goes, I'm going too.

Pa said, "Look, Al, we all don't dig, then we'll all have to go."

From the mattress where Rose of Sharon lay covered up there came a quick sharp cry, cut off in the middle. Ma whirled and went to her. Rose of Sharon was holding her breath. Her eyes were filled with terror.

Mrs. Wainwright came into the car. "Look!" Ma pointed at Rose of Sharon's face. Her teeth were clamped on her lower lip and her forehead wet with sweat, and the shining terror was in her eyes. "I think it's come," Ma said. "It's early."

The girl heaved a great sigh and relaxed. She released her lip and closed her eyes. Mrs. Wainwright bent over her.

"Did it kinda grab you all over—quick? Open up an' answer me." Rose of Sharon nodded weakly. Mrs. Wainwright turned to Ma. "Yep," she said. "It's come. Early, you say?"

"She's had a cold. Maybe the fever brought it."

"Well, she ought to be up an' walking around."

"She can't," Ma said. "She ain't got the strength."

"Well, she ought to." Mrs. Wainwright grew quiet and stern with efficiency. "I helped with lots of babies," she said. "Come on, let's close that door. Keep out the draft." The two women pushed on the heavy sliding door. "I'll get our lamp, too," Mrs. Wainwright said. Her face was purple with excitement. "Aggie," she called. "You take care of these here little fellows."

Ma nodded. "That's right. Ruthie! You an' Winfield get down with Aggie. Go on now."

"Why?" they demanded.

"Cause Rosasharn gonna have her baby."

The women helped Rose of Sharon to her feet and pinned a blanket over her shoulders. Then Ma held her arm from one side, and Mrs. Wainwright from the other. They turned slowly and walked her back, over and over. And the rain drummed deeply on the roof.

Pa stuck his head in through the narrow opening. His hat dripped with water. "What you shut the door for?" he asked. And then he saw the walking women.

Ma said, "Her time's come."

"Then we got to build that bank."

"You got to."

Pa sloshed through the mud to the stream. Twenty men stood in the rain. Pa cried, "We got to build her. My girl got her pains." And 20 men worked through the night in the rain to stem the rising waters.

Rose of Sharon screamed fiercely under the pains. For a long time the screams continued from the car, and at last they were still.

Pa returned to the boxcar. The two lamps were turned low. Ma sat on the mattress beside Rose of Sharon, fanning the girl's still face with a piece of cardboard. Mrs. Wainwright poked dry brush into the stove, and a dank smoke edged out. Ma looked up at Pa, and then quickly down.

Mrs. Wainwright left her work and came to Pa. She pulled him by the elbow to the corner of the car. She picked up a lantern and held it over an apple box in the corner. On a newspaper lay a blue shriveled mummy.

"Never breathed," said Mrs. Wainwright softly. "Never was alive." She picked up a sack and covered the apple box.

Pa said, "We done what we could."

"I know," Ma said.

"Did we slip up?" he pleaded. "Is there anything we

could of did?"

"Don't take no blame. Hush. It'll be all right."

Ma folded her hands in her lap, and her tired eyes never left the face of Rose of Sharon, sleeping in exhaustion. And Pa and Al and Uncle John sat in the car doorway and watched the steely dawn come.

In the gray dawn light, Uncle John carried a shovel in one hand and the apple box under his arm to a place where the boiling stream ran close to the road, where the willows grew along the roadside. The rain had stopped, but the sky was deep and solid with cloud. For a time he stood watching the swift water swirl by. He put the shovel down. And then he leaned over and set the box in the stream and steadied it with his hand.

He said fiercely, "Go down an' tell them. Go down in the street an' rot an' tell them that way. That's the way you can talk. Don't even know if you was a boy or a girl. Ain't gonna find out. Go on down an' lay in the street. Maybe they'll know then."

He guided the box gently out into the current and let it go. It settled low in the water, edged sideways, whirled around, and turned slowly over. Uncle John grabbed the shovel and went rapidly back to the box-cars.

The waters continued to rise. Ma said, "It's time. We're getting out of here, getting to higher ground."

The Joads moved up across the highway. Ma and Pa half dragged the weakened Rose of Sharon along. The rain poured down in sheets. Far off, a blackened barn stood. "Look!" Ma said. "I bet it's dry in that barn." It was dark inside. A little light came in through the cracks between the boards.

Ma looked into gloom and saw two figures; a man

who lay on his back, and a boy sitting beside him. The boy got up slowly and came toward her. His voice croaked, "You own this here?"

"No," Ma said. "Just come in out of the wet. We got a sick girl here." Then, "What's the matter with him?"

"He's starving. He ain't eaten for six days."

Ma and Rose of Sharon looked deep into each other's eyes. The girl's breath came short and gasping.

"Yes," she said.

Ma smiled. "I knowed you would. I knowed!"

Rose of Sharon hoisted her tired body up and drew her blanket about her. She moved slowly to the corner and stood looking down at the man's wasted face, into his wide, frightened eyes. Then slowly she lay down beside him. He shook his head slowly from side to side. Rose of Sharon loosened one side of her blanket and bared herself. "You got to," she said. She moved closer and pulled his head close. "There!" she said. "There." Her hand moved behind his head and supported it. Her fingers moved gently in his hair. She looked up and across the barn, and her lips came together and smiled mysteriously.

REVIEWING YOUR READING

CHAPTER 1

FINDING THE MAIN IDEA

1. The most important point in this chapter is that

   (A) people wear goggles to protect their eyes   (B) men lose their puzzled look and become angry   (C) men sit in their doorways thinking   (D) dust storms destroy the land of Oklahoma.

REMEMBERING DETAILS

2. The crop that is destroyed is

   (A) wheat   (B) carrots   (C) corn   (D) oats.

DRAWING CONCLUSIONS

3. We can guess that the farmers

   (A) will just plant new crops   (B) will have to pipe in water from another state   (C) will not be affected by the dust storms   (D) will suffer greatly because of the dust storms.

USING YOUR REASON

4. The dust storms are so frightening because

   (A) the farmers will lose their farms if the dust storms destroy their crops   (B) the people are afraid of the dark   (C) the dust brings disease   (D) the dust covers everything.

IDENTIFYING THE MOOD

5. The overall feeling in this chapter can best be described as

   (A) happy   (B) desperate   (C) foolish   (D) silly.

THINKING IT OVER

6. Do you think the personal relationships among family members are important to the people in this chapter? Find evidence in the text to support your answer.

CHAPTER 2

FINDING THE MAIN IDEA

1. The main event in this chapter is

(A) Tom Joad hitches a ride home after being released from prison
(B) a truck driver breaks the "No Riders" rule   (C) Tom Joad's
clothes are cheap and new   (D) Tom Joad hasn't spoken to his
family in a while.

REMEMBERING DETAILS

2. Tom Joad's age is

    (A) about 45   (B) about 18   (C) less than 30   (D) 40.

3. Tom Joad had been in prison for the crime of

    (A) bank robbery   (B) fraud   (C) embezzlement   (D) homicide.

DRAWING CONCLUSIONS

4. From the description of Tom Joad's hands, we can guess that he

    (A) is a writer   (B) has been doing a lot of manual labor
    (C) has been working in a library   (D) is an actor.

USING YOUR REASON

5. The truck driver tells Tom to stay on the running board until they
    get to the bend because

    (A) he's playing a joke on Tom   (B) he is really cruel
    (C) he doesn't want anyone to see that he's picking up a hitchhiker
    (D) he needs to clear off the front seat first, and he doesn't want to
    waste any time.

IDENTIFYING THE MOOD

6. The truck driver's attitude can best be described as

    (A) curious   (B) kind   (C) depressed   (D) affectionate.

THINKING IT OVER

7. Based on what you know so far about Tom Joad and about the
    situation in Oklahoma, what do you think will happen when Tom
    gets home?

CHAPTER 3

FINDING THE MAIN IDEA

1. The most important thing that happens in Chapter 3 is

    (A) Tom meets Jim Casy   (B) Jim Casy tells Tom he no longer has
    the calling   (C) Tom finds out that his family is moving west
    (D) Muley Graves says he won't leave the land.

REMEMBERING DETAILS

2. Tom offers Jim Casey a drink of

   (A) soda (B) water (C) coffee (D) whiskey.

DRAWING CONCLUSIONS

3. The fact that the family is heading west means that

   (A) they probably lost the farm (B) Tom's father has been offered a good job in California (C) the family wants to get away from Tom (D) they will be living on the beach.

IDENTIFYING THE MOOD

4. The description of the Joad house suggests a feeling of

   (A) hope (B) neglect (C) joy (D) excitement.

THINKING IT OVER

5. Look back at the section on page 15 that begins, "The owner men" and ends on page 16 with, "to figure, to wonder." Notice that the Joads are not mentioned here. Why do you think the author includes this section in the story?

CHAPTER 4

FINDING THE MAIN IDEA

1. The main event in Chapter 4 is that

   (A) the Joads leave for California (B) Rose of Sharon is pregnant (C) Noah is strange (D) Ma is happy to see Tom.

REMEMBERING DETAILS

2. At Uncle John's, Granma and Grampa sleep in

   (A) the living room (B) the master bedroom (C) the barn (D) the backyard.

USING YOUR REASON

3. Ma is not so sure everything will be fine in California because

   (A) it sounds too good to be true (B) she's heard some bad stories from people who went there and came back (C) she always looks on the bad side of things (D) she can predict the future.

98

IDENTIFYING THE MOOD

4. Look back at the first four paragraphs of this chapter. The salesmen seem to view their customers as

   (A) victims to be taken advantage of (B) equals who deserve to get a good deal (C) people who are out to cheat the salesmen (D) fellow human beings in need of help.

THINKING IT OVER

5. What kind of person do you think Ma Joad is? Use evidence from the text to support your answer.

CHAPTER 5

FINDING THE MAIN IDEA

1. The main issue in Chapter 5 is that

   (A) the trip to California is difficult (B) the car breaks down (C) the family has to pay 50 cents to sleep at a campground (D) the dog gets run over.

REMEMBERING DETAILS

2. Grampa dies of

   (A) a heart attack (B) food poisoning (C) injuries suffered when he is hit by a car (D) a stroke.

DRAWING CONCLUSIONS

3. Based on the gas station owner's reaction to the Joads, we can assume that

   (A) his experiences with the migrants have not been good (B) he is a cruel man (C) he will cheat them (D) he doesn't like dogs.

USING YOUR REASON

4. The reason Ma says that Tom will be committing a crime as soon as he crosses the state line is that

   (A) she knows he will rob a store as soon as he can (B) he is on parole and is not allowed to leave the state (C) she just doesn't trust him (D) his driver's license is good only in Oklahoma.

THINKING IT OVER

5. Why do you think the growers in California might advertise for

more workers than they really need? Use evidence from the text to support your answer.

CHAPTER 6

FINDING THE MAIN IDEA

1. The main thing that happens in this chapter is that

   (A) Sairy Wilson gets too sick to continue traveling   (B) the Joads make it to California   (C) Noah decides to stay by the river (D) Granma dies.

REMEMBERING DETAILS

2. By the time the family gets to California, they have

   (A) $100   (B) a few dollars   (C) about $40   (D) no money.

3. Some people who are on their way back to Texas tell the Joads that they will soon be called

   (A) bums   (B) vagrants   (C) thieves   (D) Okies.

DRAWING CONCLUSIONS

4. The Joads keep traveling west, despite all the bad reports about California, because

   (A) it's no better for them in Oklahoma   (B) they don't believe the stories   (C) they don't have much sense   (D) they feel that they owe it to Granma and Grampa.

IDENTIFYING THE MOOD

5. Reread the second-to-last paragraph of this chapter. The description of the scenery as the Joads drive down the hill into the valley sets a mood of

   (A) sorrow   (B) hope   (C) humor   (D) despair.

THINKING IT OVER

6. Why do you think Steinbeck chose to have Granma and Grampa die before the family reached California? Do you think there is something symbolic about the fact that they died during the trip? Why or why not?

CHAPTER 7

FINDING THE MAIN IDEA

1. The most important thing that happens in this chapter is that
   (A) Tom trips the deputy (B) Connie and Rose of Sharon argue
   (C) Connie Rivers disappears (D) Rose of Sharon sheds some
   tears.

REMEMBERING DETAILS

2. The name given to the migrant settlements near the edges of many
   towns is
   (A) Tent City (B) Skid Row (C) Hooverville (D) Edgetown.

3. Rose of Sharon wanted Connie to learn about
   (A) computers (B) airplanes (C) car repair (D) radios.

DRAWING CONCLUSIONS

4. When Connie disappears, it is most likely that he has
   (A) deserted Rose of Sharon (B) gone ahead to find a better place
   for the family to live (C) found work and has not had time to tell
   the family (D) been put in jail.

USING YOUR REASON

5. The reason Jim Casy has a faint smile on his face when he is
   arrested is that he
   (A) is confused (B) is thinking of a joke (C) feels as if he's
   doing something good (D) knows he's fooling the arresting
   officers.

IDENTIFYING THE MOOD

6. Just before Jim Casy kicks the deputy in the neck, the mood is one
   of
   (A) fun (B) sadness (C) danger (D) happiness.

THINKING IT OVER

7. Put yourself in Connie Rivers's place. What are your options?
   What would you do, given those options?

CHAPTER 8

FINDING THE MAIN IDEA

1. The main point of this chapter is that

    (A) the family is in a decent place now   (B) Rose of Sharon is getting bigger   (C) Ma promises to take care of Rose of Sharon   (D) Ma is able to relax.

REMEMBERING DETAILS

2. The entertainment on Saturday night is

    (A) a country music show   (B) a movie   (C) a jazz trio   (D) a dance.

DRAWING CONCLUSIONS

3. The reason the members of the Farmers' Association don't like the government camps is that

    (A) the camps occupy good farming land   (B) they don't want the workers to get used to good treatment   (C) they're just jealous   (D) the people who run the government camp make sure that the workers get good wages.

USING YOUR REASON

4. During the dance, the shrill whistle is

    (A) the signal for the police to break up the dance   (B) a bird   (C) a bird watcher   (D) a train.

IDENTIFYING THE MOOD

5. The overall mood at the government camp is one of

    (A) depression   (B) happiness   (C) terror   (D) wealth.

THINKING IT OVER

6. Why doesn't the government turn every Hooverville into a camp like the one described in Chapter 8?

CHAPTER 9

FINDING THE MAIN IDEA

1. The main thing that happens in this chapter is that

    (A) Jim Casy is killed and Tom gets revenge   (B) the family picks peaches for five cents a box   (C) the rate for picking peaches drops to two and a half cents   (D) Tom gets hit in the head.

REMEMBERING DETAILS

2. Jim Casy's "crime" is

   (A) stealing peaches   (B) leading a strike   (C) selling drugs
   (D) armed robbery.

3. On its first day of picking peaches, the family earns

   (A) 5 dollars   (B) 20 cents   (C) 1 dollar   (D) nothing.

DRAWING CONCLUSIONS

4. The Joads leave the government camp because

   (A) they don't like the residents   (B) they want to see the rest of
   California   (C) they can't find enough work near there   (D) Tom's
   parole officer is after him.

USING YOUR REASON

5. Organizing a strike, the way Jim Casy does, is dangerous because

   (A) it's against the law   (B) no one likes a union organizer
   (C) the owners of the farms don't like union organizers
   (D) Tom's parole officer is after him.

IDENTIFYING THE MOOD

6. As the Joads leave the camp the day after Jim Casy's death, the
   mood in the truck can best be described as

   (A) tense   (B) adventurous   (C) fun   (D) joyful.

THINKING IT OVER

7. The price of fresh produce is so low that the small growers are
   losing money. They cannot even get the fruit picked for the amount
   they get for the fruit. Food is destroyed, while people go hungry. If
   you were President of the United States, what would you do about
   this problem?

CHAPTER 10

FINDING THE MAIN IDEA

1. The main idea in the last scene of the book is that

   (A) the poor help the poor   (B) the starving man was frightened
   (C) Rose of Sharon and Ma finally make up after their quarrel

(D) Rose of Sharon smiled mysteriously.

REMEMBERING DETAILS

2. When Tom has to leave, Ma insists on giving him

    (A) a bag full of food   (B) seven dollars   (C) a warm coat
    (D) a hug and a kiss.

3. Tom has to leave because

    (A) Winfield told a friend what Tom had done   (B) Ruthie told
    another girl what Tom had done   (C) Rose of Sharon wants him to
    find Connie   (D) there is not enough food for him.

DRAWING CONCLUSIONS

4. Based on what Tom says about Jim Casy, we can assume that Tom
    plans to become a

    (A) preacher   (B) teacher   (C) union organizer   (D) police officer.

USING YOUR REASON

5. We can guess that the reason Rose of Sharon loses her baby is that

    (A) her diet has not been very good   (B) no doctor was there to
    help with the delivery   (C) she is too young to have a baby
    (D) she is too old to have a baby.

IDENTIFYING THE MOOD

6. Tom's mood when he was explaining his plans to Ma can be
    described as

    (A) angry   (B) hopeful   (C) desperate   (D) fearful.

THINKING IT OVER

7. Do you think Tom Joad will ever see his family again? Explain
    your answer.